The Spirits Have Nothing to Do with Us

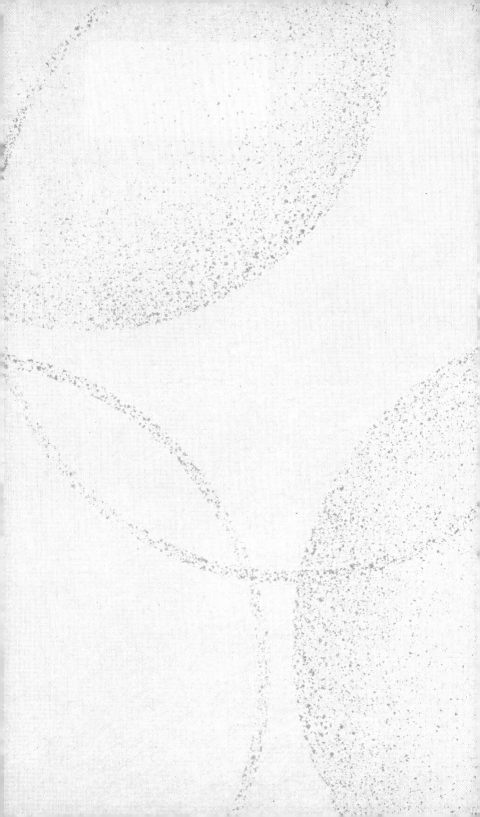

THE SPIRITS
HAVE NOTHING
TO DO WITH US

NEW CHINESE CANADIAN
FICTION

edited by

DAN K. WOO

Published by Buckrider Books
an imprint of Wolsak and Wynn Publishers
280 James Street North
Hamilton, ON L8R2L3
www.wolsakandwynn.ca

Editor for Buckrider Books: Paul Vermeersch | Copy editor: Jennifer Hale
Cover and interior design: Michel Vrana
Cover image: *Roaming outer space in an airship,* Zhang Ruiheng (张瑞恒), Landsberger collection, International Institute of Social History, Amsterdam
Typeset in Garamond Premier Pro
Printed by Rapido Books, Montreal, Canada

The publisher gratefully acknowledges the support of the Ontario Arts Council, the Canada Council for the Arts and the Government of Canada.

Library and Archives Canada Cataloguing in Publication
Title: The spirits have nothing to do with us : new Chinese Canadian fiction / edited by Dan K. Woo.
Names: Woo, Dan K., editor.
Description: Short stories.
Identifiers: Canadiana 20230224857 | ISBN 9781989496671 (softcover)
Subjects: LCSH: Short stories, Canadian—21st century. | CSH: Canadian literature (English)—Chinese Canadian authors | CSH: Short stories, Canadian (English)—21st century Classification: LCC PS8323.C5 S65 2022 | DDC C813/.0108951—dc23

汪怡清

For Isabella Wang

Contents

Introduction · Dan K. Woo / 9

上 CHINESE

Lonely Face Club · Bingji Ye,
translated by Dan K. Woo / 15

下 CANADIAN

Moonlight in the Palm of My Hand
· Ellen Chang-Richardson / 65

Coal Flowers · Isabella Wang / 71

Egg Tart, Deconstructed · Eddy Boudel Tan / 83

Fault Lines · Yilin Wang / 89

The Best Ham and Egg Sandwich on the Island
· Sam Cheuk / 105

Red Egg and Ginger · Anna Ling Kaye / 109

July Has Nothing to Do with Gods · Sheung-King / 127

Foggy Days, Foggy Ways · Lydia Kwa / 137

Editor's Note / 147

Contributor Biographies / 149

Introduction

AS OTHERS HAVE OBSERVED ELSEWHERE IN THE WORLD, short stories have seen a shift from "the mythic to the anecdotal," from impersonal storytelling where the narrator has a minor or invisible role to "storytelling that is intensely personal, self-conscious, and narrated with a distinctive 'voice.'"[1] Canadian short fiction has seen the same shift over the last two or three decades, and these "voices" today are increasingly representative of an alternative worldview.

Whether ethnic, Indigenous, trans or other marginalized identities, this literary shift reflects the changing makeup of Canadian readership as much as the changing talent pool from which Canadian writers emerge. Among this broad range of voices, Chinese Canadian writers, like other identity groups, have sought their share of space as well, speaking to their specific readers. These

---

1   Joyce Carol Oates, preface to *The Oxford Book of American Short Stories*, 2nd ed. (New York: Oxford University Press, 2012).

writers are less preoccupied with retelling immigrant stories or upholding minority myths.

More than before, we expect, as readers, a flourishing of literary activity from Canadian publishers. A wider range of marketable stories, character archetypes, nuances of emotion, relationships and love stories. Even literary diversity in China, for example, supposedly smothered under the suffocating ideology of Communism, constantly surprises. In China, odious and manufactured oppression may exist in other forms certainly, but not in this particular form – market forces that centre white readership.

In Canada, change is happening. This collection brings together Chinese Canadian writers who are actively working on a new kind of writing that expresses and centres their own experience, writing for a readership that they define for themselves.

In the first story of this collection, the main character Xia Ling laments about, aptly enough, being stereotyped by her lover. "These prejudices always made Xia Ling unhappy, but she didn't want to defend herself. What was the point? You can't explain it to every person. The best answer was to try hard to turn one's own situation around."

Exquisite Chinese language writing is all around us, just waiting for us to enjoy it. We only need to find the courage to open the pages. Translation plays a critical role in the development of Canadian literature – this is why roughly half the anthology is balanced by translated work; in this case, "Lonely Face Club," by Bingji Ye, a writer virtually unknown in Canada, now available in translation for the first time.[2]

Two poets in this collection, writing prose here, make similar observations. In "Moonlight in the Palm of My Hand," Ellen Chang-Richardson hints at a difficult truth: "We'd sat over there:

---

2   As translated by the editor.

by the man-made pond in the man-made park in our man-made compound." That is – we are all in a prison of our own making, and we don't realize it until it's too late. Isabella Wang shows us in "Coal Flowers" that, in the face of adversity, life has no choice but to continue: "I looked at the men. Their faces were as expressionless and unreadable as the sky. Mr. Hong sent me home after that. My training started on Monday."

In Eddy Boudel Tan's story, "Egg Tart, Deconstructed," a young couple dines in a fancy restaurant, an evening that ends in an unexpected way. We learn that, while the egg tart has been reinvented, the emotions remain hidden.

Yilin Wang reaches into present-day China to reveal "Fault Lines" – her own take on the schisms, tensions and deep hurt that bubbles and boils under the surface of everyday, mundane life: "Who did he think he was, pushing her around? But she didn't fling his hand off her shoulder, only squeezed her fist into a ball and kept walking." The relationships dissected in her story, between boy and girl, between grandmother and granddaughter, between father and child, are beautifully and confidently wrought, and equally painful to read.

In "The Best Ham and Egg Sandwich on the Island," Sam Cheuk, also a poet, tries to reclaim his own vision of memory and childhood: "No one would know the eatery was there if you're not from Pok Fu Lam, tucked away beside the village social club, with a barely legible sign." Cheuk tells us about the shop, and the proprietor, in his distinctive voice – and there is an intimacy and sentimentality in his descriptions that often evades outside observers trying to capture Hong Kong's peculiar type of modernity.

In Anna Ling Kaye's "Red Egg and Ginger," food entices us. "The candy sweetness gives way to the fiery root beneath, and Mei holds it in her mouth without chewing. Ginger children bouncing up and down on her tongue until she can't take it anymore and spits them into her palm." And yet, it's not food we are reading about.

"July Has Nothing to Do with Gods" shows us Sheung-King in ideal form – a sort of Kowloon Cinesphere that pulls together a world we have never seen before and makes it dance before our eyes.

Finally, in "Foggy Days, Foggy Ways," Lydia Kwa shares an atmospheric tale of what life has been like for so many, by capturing a feeling we all know well. She teaches us that the end is but a beginning, a release to adventure, some beautiful new world we are on the verge of exploring. Even the youngest of us are brave explorers.

The stories in this collection, all written by Chinese Canadians who currently reside in Canada, represent authors who have already begun creating bodies of work that show a more honest depiction of what Chinese and Chinese Canadian individuals – and writers – are like.

– Dan K. Woo
Toronto, March 2022

Chinese

Lonely Face Club

Bingji Ye

TRANSLATED BY DAN K. WOO

I

IN XIA LING'S MEMORY, H WAS A GREY CITY.

This winter was particularly long. It was already February, and still so cold. In the dense dusk, the air felt wet and heavy in one's mouth, forcing each breath into a gasp. The setting sun had disappeared early, hiding from the biting cold.

The weather forecast said there would be heavy snow tonight.

Over the last twenty years, the street scene underwent earth-shaking changes. There were now row upon row of tall buildings on both sides. In these rows of magnificent buildings, a visitor could find several small red-brick European-style buildings left over from the war against Japan. The protruding semicircular balconies were still the same as before, with white curtains hanging inside. Grey pillars stood on both sides of the balcony, unobtrusive, graceful, silently telling stories about that bloody era. Xia Ling knew that it was not easy for these buildings to be preserved. Through the decades, when the big hands of provincial and municipal leaders were drawing up blueprints on the map, these buildings must have been carefully and lovingly protected. Only by this method could these old buildings exist and bear witness to the ancient history of the city.

Twenty-nine Chenyang Road. That's right, this was the place. Xia Ling looked up at the plaque on the side of the road: LONELY FACE CLUB. The glass on the window was clean, faintly reflecting the figure of a woman in a white leather coat gathered at the waist and silver-grey boots. She had long curly chestnut hair, fair skin and delicate makeup.

It was seven o'clock. The evening was just beginning, and there were many people inside Lonely Face. Right next to her was a huge poster with a picture of a slender woman dancing with smoky red hair covering her entire face. She was the host tonight – DJ Pony.

At such cold temperatures, people on the street hurriedly walked by, either ducking into a restaurant or getting into a taxi while breathing hot air into their hands. No one stayed still like Xia Ling. After a while, Xia Ling's feet were numb from cold. Lifting her wrist to look at the time, she saw there was still half an hour. Each breath of the blue bitter air brought pain to her body. After all the heartache she had experienced, in another half-hour, she would see him.

Xia Ling looked into the bar through the window. The night-club remained faintly the same as it had been twenty years ago: dim yellow lights, long and narrow wooden corridors, island bar counters and two rows of clean goblets within reach above the bar. The difference was that the people inside were no longer the faces of those people back then. At that time it was not called Lonely Face but Blues Bar, the largest nightclub in the city. Eighteen-year-old Xia Ling had started working there after finishing high school. An older girl from her hometown introduced her to the Blues Bar. New employees with no experience could not sell foreign wines, which had a higher commission. She could only sell domestic beer. In the winter of the year she turned twenty,

Xia Ling was finally qualified to sell foreign wines. As it was, Xia Ling used most of her monthly income to fund the studies of her two younger brothers.

In this city of long winters, people liked to eat from boiling hot pots. They came to the bar in groups to drink and sing.

He often came alone, sitting at a small table near the stage and ordering two plates of snacks along with a bottle of whisky. He had a strong palate and never diluted the whisky with any drink. Sometimes, he would show up already inebriated, having obviously drunk at dinner. After sitting down, he would add two pieces of ice to the amber whisky. There were also a few times when he used the private karaoke room with a large group of friends. But among the singers, he had always been just a listener.

Xia Ling paid attention to all these details, not just because of his burly figure, the dark blue suit, the Motorola phone in his hand, the Rolex on his wrist and the expensive cigarettes he was holding, but also because of the focused stillness in which he listened to the songs. That kind of silence meant one's body had turned into a feather and floated off to a place where few people go. Only at this moment would his eyebrows relax. Whenever Xia Ling saw the smooth centre between his eyebrows, she would feel the bottom of her heart inexplicably soften, like a delicate catkin falling on the tip of the sun's wings. Later, she even saved him the seat he used to sit in and led other guests elsewhere. If he was slightly drunk when he came, she would add ice to his alcohol before serving it. Every time, he would smile approvingly at her. His sideburns had already begun to turn pale, but his smile was full of youthful energy.

At this moment, the softness in Xia Ling's heart was like the horizon in the twilight dusk, spreading to her cheeks unknowingly. She swiped her phone – there were fifteen minutes left. Fifteen long minutes. She almost suffocated from nervousness.

The night was getting darker. There were more people on the streets.

Today was Valentine's Day in the West. Girls with fresh young faces clutched roses to their breasts, skipping about everywhere, happiness hanging on the corners of their slightly upturned lips, so full the joy almost dripped down. Lonely Xia Ling felt a little cold, but she was reluctant to go in and wait. If she could see him coming across the road from a distance, it would be worthwhile to be able to watch for a few more seconds. Although she hadn't seen him in twenty years, Xia Ling knew that she would recognize him immediately. As long as he came to the appointment tonight, as long as he remembered the agreement they had made with each other. As long as he was still alive . . .

The weather was so cold, but her hand – which held her phone – was sweating slightly. Even though she was forty years old, she felt like a jittery young girl, how come? She steadied her mind and opened WeChat, only to find a new friend request. It was a stranger with the nickname "Autumn Rain," who wanted to say hello. The profile picture was a scene of West Lake in the rain. Gender: male.

Xia Ling looked at her WeChat profile photo: a face beautified by the phone camera, her complexion clear and milky, her cheeks like peach blossoms, her pretty eyes casting a beguiling glance. It could stand up to any comparison.

She had time on her hands. If someone wanted to chat with her a bit, it would calm her mind down. Xia Ling casually clicked "Accept."

2

"Hello there."

The other party immediately typed two words. Xia Ling liked the full stop after "Hello there," a feeling of beginning and end. Unlike *him*, who had sent no news. A goodbye that lasted twenty years.

Over the past two decades, China's communications industry had developed rapidly. Xia Ling remembered that her first device was a pager, the expensive kind that supported Chinese characters, not like the cheap kind that could only receive phone numbers. It was a Motorola pager bought from the wholesale market, with a streamlined black shell, small and exquisite. She searched the electronic wholesale market for a store that had low prices and bought it for sixteen hundred yuan. The moment she bought it, Xia Ling wrote to her family, leaving her call number with her mother. That pager was like the string to a kite, and Xia Ling asked her mother to hold it firmly and never let go.

The employees in the bar changed frequently, like a revolving lantern. Xia Ling remembered that day clearly. She had placed her expensive pager in her bag and then hung the bag under her clothes in the locker room. At the end of her shift, the pager had disappeared. Xia Ling's heart froze. She paged herself dozens of times, but the locker room was silent. Where? Where? Where did it go?! It was the busy harvesting season. Father sick with a stubborn cough. Two younger brothers busy with homework. Mother was alone taking care of three acres of fields. How could Xia Ling not worry, how could she continue normally? Now that the pager was gone, and the kite line between herself and her home was broken, Xia Ling felt an emptiness in her chest.

She thought about it. Xiao Jing was the primary suspect for stealing the pager. Jing was a new employee, a couple of years younger than her. Jing was not tall, rather plain-looking, but had full breasts, making her more attractive in her work clothes. Perhaps because she was a newcomer, or perhaps out of jealousy, she was often sent to clean the washroom by the madam of the establishment, who was the boss's lover. The washroom was characteristically dirty, a dark epitome of the city. Frequently one could find all kinds of vomit. Because Jing was awkward, not pretty, earning a low commission, she looked more like a janitor. In addition to cleaning up different kinds of excretions, Jing also for the first time saw used condoms, syringes and cheap torn women's underwear there.

Whenever she saw something new, Jing would whisper to Xia Ling. At first she spoke shyly and excitedly. A few months later, the expression on Jing's face had changed into something else: disdain. Xia Ling listened with the same patience, without interrupting, without expression, hiding her knowing smile.

Maybe it was because Xia Ling knew what Jing was going through.

It was after a certain incident, one evening, that Jing and Xia Ling became intimate friends who talked about everything.

It was an early autumn evening. The autumn breeze was cool, and the leaves were still dense. Through the shade of the trees, the moon was hanging high and elegant, emitting refreshingly bright golden rays.

The Blues Bar liquor salesgirls were still wearing summer uniforms: a close-fitting white short-sleeved shirt and a very short black hip skirt. Someone in the private room that Jing was looking after had probably drunk too much. *Pop!* That was the sound of a bottle breaking. Xia Ling happened to pass by, and her heart tensed up. In her experience, this was a sign of a gang fight. She called security staff on her headset and then pushed open the door to the private room.

The private room was peaceful, no tense atmosphere at all. A bottle of beer was shattered on the floor. Jing had a stack of napkins in her hand and was squatting to wipe the floor. She had already cleaned up the broken bottle fragments, and no broken glass could be seen. Xia Ling was surprised to see that he was sitting in the middle of the sofa, with a cigarette between his fingers. Seeing him there, Xia Ling felt a little relieved – he wouldn't just sit back and watch if something off-putting had happened. Next to him was a dark, voluminous man in his early forties, wearing a pair of gold-rimmed glasses, whom everyone called "Gold." Gold was eating slices of watermelon with a toothpick and saying with a strange smile on his face, "Meimei, come. There is watermelon juice all over the floor. Come and wipe here."

"Ai," Jing replied. She squatted at the person's feet and wiped the floor with a napkin. Her skirt was already short, and this posture exposed the curve of Jing's hip. Gold's eyes quickly shot into Jing's neckline. He raised his crossed leg just at the right moment and rubbed Jing's ass with his foot as if unintentionally. "Meimei, I haven't seen you before. What's your name?"

Jing stood up as if she'd had an electric shock, embarrassed. When Xia Ling saw this, she pulled Jing back. "Brother, are you not happy with our drinks and you have a problem? Why smash the beer bottle?" She poked Jing, while saying, "Go, bring two more beers, and get a mop to clean up the floor." Jing understood and slipped out of the room.

Seeing this, Gold uncrossed his legs dejectedly, handing a slice of watermelon to the man next to him. "Executive Yue, come, have a piece of watermelon."

Executive Yue. Xia Ling secretly noted it in her heart. This Executive Yue had been leaning back on the sofa, smoking a cigarette unhurriedly, looking at the picture in the jukebox, his face blank, as if all this had nothing to do with him. From this, Xia Ling understood that the romantic stories of heroic gentlemen saving beauties in distress could only appear in TV dramas.

In reality, the world was full of deadly traps. Once you are in a dangerous situation, you have to calm down and find a way to get out of it yourself. As for girls who work in such a precarious environment, the greatest wisdom is not to put themselves in danger in the first place.

Since that incident, Jing's name for Xia Ling changed from "Sister Xia" to "Sis," and they became close enough companions to chat in the bathroom together.

"Sis, how many people do you share your apartment with now? Can I come live with you? We can go home together after getting off work."

"Sure! When does your rental lease finish? Move into my place when it expires. Let's buy a bunk bed and share my room."

Xia Ling bought a skirt. Jing put it up against her body happily. "It's too long. If I grow as tall as you, it would be fine."

Xia Ling bought a lipstick. Xiao Jing also put it on her lips in front of the mirror. "Sis, is this too red? It's like having eaten a child."

Xia Ling bought a pager. Jing held it in her hands, looking at it from the left and from the right, pressing the buttons back and forth. She couldn't put it down. "Sis, I want to buy one too . . . But it's more than sixteen hundred yuan. Apart from paying the rent, I can't buy meat more than a few times a month. Besides . . . I don't have any use for it."

Under the dim light, the pager screen glowed with a pale green light. The plastic sheet on the screen had not yet been removed. Xia Ling couldn't bear to take it off; she liked its brand-new appearance.

"Jing, give my number to your family in your hometown. If they ever want to find you, they can call me. Anyway, we are always together," Xia Ling said as she took the pager from Jing's hand, put it in the inner pocket of her purse and zipped it up.

Except for Jing, no one knew that Xia Ling had bought a pager. And the next day, Jing disappeared from the Blues Bar. No one knew where she had gone.

"Are you alone?"

The stranger Xia Ling had just added to WeChat sent another greeting.

"Alone." Xia Ling left her thoughts in the grey past and returned to reality.

"Me too . . ."

"Today is Valentine's Day. You should be with your lover."

Xia Ling didn't know how many times she had seen this kind of pickup line, but it didn't matter to her now. Loneliness was an excuse to strike up a conversation with only one purpose. If she liked his looks, she would not refuse him on a day like today. She only hoped he was not married, because she did not want the complications of a family man. She had tasted the pungency of loneliness, the bitterness of the dark night. She could hardly remember how she was able to tear off such loneliness and swallow it piece by piece. She felt her inner self grow stronger each time she tossed and turned, watching the sky gradually reveal a blue-purple light, turning redder and redder until it finally became the rising sun. Gradually, loneliness no longer caused sadness and became something she played with in her palm to enliven her life.

After a while Autumn Rain responded. "It's been almost three years since the divorce, and now I am lonely."

Xia Ling smiled slightly, and the peach cheeks hidden by her hair suddenly turned into a freshly baked butter cake. The softness of her delicate skin was not at all aggressive, but it had already entangled a man's heart in a web. She deliberately and casually wrote and deleted meaningless words in the dialogue box, and was silent for a long time. She knew that the mysterious man would see "Typing . . ." displayed, and would be held in suspense, waiting to see what she would write. She didn't say a word. She knew he would finally ask, unable to hold back any longer.

"How about you? How about your husband?" As expected. Xia Ling's rose-coloured fingertips seemed to be fragrant, and she replied with a few words. "Well, husband . . . How do you know that I have a husband? Can't I be a Qi Tian leftover?"

"What is Qi Tian leftover?" he asked.

"Just an old girl who can't get married."

The other party was silent, seemingly scared off by her words, and didn't reply for a long time.

Xia Ling didn't feel the slightest loss in her heart. In the game of love, just as she didn't want to be involved with married men, every man she met didn't want to be entangled with leftover, unmarried women. Human psychology is so strange. Forty-year-old unmarried Xia Ling had long learned to do whatever she wanted in a helpless situation.

A harmless chat with a stranger could be broken off at any time, just like a casual romance. You could leave without waiting for dawn or saying goodbye.

Sensing that the mysterious man had slipped off, Xia Ling stuffed the phone into her pocket, greedily pressing her fingertips against the back of the phone, reluctant to let the warmth go.

Yes, it was too cold. Looking up at the sky, there was an eerie purple colour. Snow was on the way. Maybe it would come sooner than him.

Yue Qianshan, it's almost time. Are you dead? Why haven't you come?! Xia Ling's heart throbbed. She had been looking forward to this moment for twenty years. Now that it was close at hand, why was she so nervous? She hardly dared to look up; she was afraid of the disappointment that she would feel after looking around. She hung her head slightly, her long hair scattered in the night breeze. She felt her body shaking very badly. It must be because it was too cold, it must be. Otherwise, how could forty-year-old Xia Ling tremble like this? She hoped that at this moment someone could hug her into the depths of their arms, warm her, drive away the anxiety and whisper in her ear, "Girl, follow me."

Girl. He had once called her that.

It was during that long winter. Xia Ling, who had just started selling foreign wines, knew nothing about those dazzling products. She borrowed several books on foreign wines from the library and read them carefully. In the middle of the night, upon freshly fallen snow, she walked home, the books in a shopping bag. On the street, her shadow grew and shrank, switched from left to right and from right to left, cast by the streetlamps. Even on the coldest days, she never took a taxi, always walking home.

Xia Ling was happiest when she returned to her modest home. She took a hot bath and changed into pink cotton pyjamas patterned with Hello Kitty. She lay on the warm and comfortable bed and read thirty to fifty pages from the borrowed books. She would fall asleep whenever she felt tired. Because of her constant studying, Xia Ling quickly mastered the different types of alcohol and the techniques of mixing drinks, so that her performance surpassed the best salesgirl, and she was the champion of drink sales for many months.

At midnight one day, in order to sell a few more bottles, she wrapped herself in a silver miniskirt, showing off her curvy lines. She wore large bright purple eyeshadow and batted long, fake eyelashes. There were about twenty people in this large private room. Xia Ling thought to herself that the drink order should not be small, so she opened a bottle of twelve-year-old Chivas whisky to make a toast.

"Big brothers, I am Xia Ling. This is the first time we've met. Please look after me," Xia Ling said, handing over the business card in her hand. "It's nearly the end of the month. Please help me with my work performance. I haven't done many sales. Our team won't be able to meet our target. If we don't meet our targets for three months, we'll be wiped out by our competitors. Look at this cold weather. Where could I look for a job, right? So, I will drink to the bottom of the bottle first, out of respect. I would also like to ask you to take a few sips." She downed the amber liquid in the half-filled glass in her hand.

"Oh, this chick is pretty good. You have another glass, and we will take three more bottles."

"Really? Thank you so much. I thought to myself, the other day, I don't have enough to pay for rent for next month. But now maybe that's changed. Okay, I'll have another drink." She opened another bottle and poured a full glass.

A fiery burning sensation spread down her throat and into her stomach. She felt that her throat was about to be scorched. She hesitated, took a few breaths and drank the rest.

"Little Xia, right? How did your manager train you? We have a few lady friends in our party. Do you expect them to drink this too?" said a young man with a shaved head.

"I'm sorry, I didn't think of that. We have several very good cocktails here, low in strength, sweet and sour, good for beautifying skin. Would you like to have a few glasses to taste?" Xia Ling handed over the wine list. Baldy made a gesture to indicate that he didn't need to look at it. "Just bring them. And another bottle of red wine." A few minutes later, five cocktails and a bottle of dry red were served by the white-gloved waiter. Baldy picked up the red wine, uncorked it and poured a full glass for Xia Ling. "You can't just toast the men. As the saying goes, brothers and sisters are equal. Come and toast our ladies."

Xia Ling never expected that after drinking Chivas, she would still need to drink so much red wine, and she avoided taking up the offered glass for a long time.

Perhaps seeing Xia Ling's embarrassment, someone in the crowd tried to stop him. "Baldy, it's not easy for this salesgirl. Let it go – no need to make her drink it."

Unexpectedly, these words angered Baldy. "Damn you. You know shit! Mind your own business!"

Xia Ling immediately smiled to smooth things over. "Don't fight. Don't fight. We are out for fun. Let's not say anything that hurts each other's feelings. . . . Okay, I, Xia Ling, will sacrifice myself to keep you happy. I toast all the ladies here, I wish you eternal youth and beauty, finding priceless treasures wherever you go and meeting lovers when you return home. Everyone loves you. Flowers bloom for you. You have great courage and you have great plans. You have both wealth and good looks." After speaking, she picked up the wineglass and emptied the dark red liquid in one go.

4

Xia Ling had never drunk so much before. Amidst the noisy singing and whistling, she pushed away a hand on her thigh, she didn't know whose it was, and quickly calculated in her mind while she was still awake – tonight's drink commission would be more than two thousand yuan! Her younger brother's tuition would be covered, and she could buy another pager. This wine was worth drinking! But amidst the fervour, she covered her mouth, holding back the urge to vomit, and hurried out of the room.

Fortunately, Xia Ling was still walking steadily at this moment. She rushed to the bathroom and spit out the alcohol with her hands clutching her throat. After vomiting several times, she felt a little better. She rinsed her mouth, washed her face, panting, and looked at herself pale in the mirror. Tears welled up while she was looking at herself, and she had to lower her head and wash her face again.

Finally, unable to withstand the effects of the alcohol, she slumped on the side of the sink and closed her eyes. In her stupor, she could hear a buzzing in her ears and feel the liquor surging like a tide. It reached up her body to the tip of her head, and then hit her stomach from the top of her head. She felt like she was burning inside, but also cold. So cold that she was shivering like a leaf. She waited quietly, hoping for the waves of alcohol to fight each other and to gradually calm down. She had become accustomed to sitting in the corner and waiting to sober up slowly. She longed for the warm and comfortable quilt at home, the orange-red soft lamp beside the bed and the shower in the bathroom that could spray out crystal-clear water. She wanted to cry, cry her heart out. But looking at the ghostly figures coming and going, she swallowed back the choking in her throat. There were several waves of people coming and going in the bathroom. None of them stopped to help her.

Even half-conscious, she expected nothing else. She had become accustomed to the indifference of this place. Used to living the colourful bloom of her life stubbornly in indifference.

Eventually, she wobbled to her feet, planning to go home. As soon as she stumbled out of the door, she collided with a man.

It's him. What was he called? Executive Yue? So far, she only knew that his surname was Yue.

This was the first contact between them. He didn't push Xia Ling away but held her in his arms. Through the thin shirt, she felt his arms warm and strong.

Xia Ling smiled at him and said, "Executive Yue, thank you." But she was so drunk that she couldn't lift her head again.

"Where do you live?" Under the noise of laughter and singing, she seemed to hear him asking. However, she was too tired to answer.

In this cold and lonely city, on this winter night bloated with alcohol, it was precious to have such a pair of hands to warm oneself. This warmth was like a frightened fish – it may disappear at any time. Why would Xia Ling let it slip away?

Executive Yue told the doorman to bring his car to the doorway of the bar, as it was cold outside. She was wrapped in his arms and wrapped in his coat, her body small and thin. It was not unusual for the liquor salesgirls in the nightclub to go out with guests, so no one asked any questions. She felt him gently lower her into the passenger's seat.

She rubbed her body into the car seat quietly, and he buckled her seat belt.

She was taken to a hotel room with a big bed covered with snow-white sheets.

He helped her to the bed, turned off the light and whispered, "How did you drink yourself to this state?" Then he sat on the sofa not far away and put a cigarette to his lips.

She wanted to sleep for a while, but the strong power of alcohol didn't allow her to lie peacefully for a long time. In this hopeless darkness, it seemed as if there was a huge hand that kept spinning, pulling her mind, pulling her hair and even sucking her entire slender body into that huge vortex.

She felt her stomach turning upside down.

She murmured, "Older brother . . . I'm so dizzy, I can't lie down . . ."

In the darkness, the cigarette butt between his fingers alternated between bright and dark. Upon her words, the cigarette butt lit up suddenly, and he immediately pinched it out.

He sat beside her. "Come here, lean on me for a minute." She leaned softly in his warm arms. He put the quilt on her body. "Is that better?"

"Yeah. Hug . . ." Xia Ling snorted groggily. Xia Ling felt very warm and content at this moment.

In her memory, she hadn't been held in this way for many years. When her younger brother was born when she was five years old, she saw her parents hug him. When she was eight years old, her second brother was born, and she learned to hold him. Her parents, who worked hard every day, only poured more nagging, blame and fault into Xia Ling's ears. In a sensible way, she learned how to take care of others early, but she forgot that she was still a child.

Grass on the edge of a field will grow even if no one waters or fertilizes it. In this way, Xia Ling suddenly grew into a slim and tall and good-looking girl. She had reached that age of maturity when she was expected to help relieve her family of burden. Looking at the curvy Xia Ling, her father said to her mother, "Let Lingzi marry into a good family soon. Find a good one, and some light may cast on us in the future." Her mother said, "Let's hear what Lingzi says."

On a starry night, the parents solemnly talked to Xia Ling about her future. Xia Ling burst into tears. "Mom, I don't want to marry so early, let me go out and try to make a life on my own. I don't need to go to school, but let me go to the provincial city to see what life is like for a little while." This conversation lasted late into the night, until Xia Ling knelt down and made a solemn vow that every month she would send a thousand yuan home, and her parents nodded.

A few days later, in the morning, she went to the train station. Her mother did not come to see her off as she boarded the train to the provincial capital. She only remembered that her father put an old suitcase full of luggage on the shelf above her head and wiped away her tears with his rough and cracked hands. "Why cry? We tell you to marry someone, but you don't marry. Make some money and come back often to see us."

Over two years, Xia Ling sent the money she earned back home, but she never went home. Perhaps because she knew that the family she missed day and night might not be able to give her the slightest warmth. Like an exhausted bird, she would just stay on a branch somewhere and rest. Going home was too extravagant.

Before she knew it, she had to hold back tears. She brought her thoughts back to reality. He was there, beside her. She held her nose close to him and let his scent fill her. There was a sweet fragrance of tobacco on his coat, mixed with the smell of a warm body and the musky scent of a man.

"It smells good," she said with a smile.

"What smells good?"

"The smell on you is so good." She smiled delicately.

He didn't speak, but only held her hand, rubbing her fingers one by one, occasionally making a circle on the palm of her hand and touching it lightly. Suddenly, her heart was pounding.

"What's your name?"

"Yue Qianshan."

"Brother Yue?"

"If you want."

"How old are you?"

"Thirty-eight."

"That's great. From now on, I will have an older brother. When I was in school, I envied classmates who had brothers. Now things are different." She put her arm around his neck, slid onto his lap and smirked at him. "Brother, do I look good?"

In the dark, Xia Ling's eyes shone brightly. Black pupils stood out against the whites of her eyes, her long eyelashes hanging low, opening unexpectedly like a pair of fans. The intensity of her eyes seemed to carry a constant sadness, so soft and endless, saying so much and yet so little. Her skin reflected the colourful neon light outside the window, shimmering with a reddish, satin-like gleam. Her breathing was rapid and shallow, with the subtle aroma of wine, touching the tip of his nose. Her hair, like a tangled web, rose quietly and spread open to tighten around him again and again from all directions. Then the soft and delicate lips blossomed in the centre of the web like the petals of a flower, throbbing, trembling, pressing forward against his resistance.

He rested his hands lightly on her shoulders, got up and walked to the refrigerator. He took out a bottled drink.

"Drink this."

"What is this?"

"Green tea for hangovers."

She touched it and flinched. "It's too cold, I won't drink it."

"Girl, be obedient."

"Then feed me something first, so I won't feel so cold." She looked at him coyly with a smile. She tilted her chin up, and opened her mouth, her eyes flickering closed . . .

5

The moon rose above the willow tree. It was dusk. The congestion on the street seemed to be getting better. There was no need to look at the time. Xia Ling knew that their agreed-upon time had passed.

He hadn't come.

No, he will come, he will come. Maybe it's just a traffic jam. The city has changed so much, and now traffic is everywhere, and it is difficult to move an inch during the worst of it. Besides, if, like Xia Ling, he has been away for twenty years, there will be some unfamiliar roads when he comes back. For her it was easy to fly back from Guangzhou two days beforehand and settle comfortably into a nearby hotel. But there was no guarantee that he could do the same.

In any case, he will come, because he loves her.

Xia Ling had no doubt about this. If he didn't love her, why did he cherish her so much in the first place?

She clearly remembered how she felt when she took off her clothes in front of a man for the first time. It was like waiting for a grand inspection, without a preview. She dared not make one more move, she dared not raise her eyes directly into his eyes. She dared not breathe. Fortunately, the darkness of the night was like a fig leaf; otherwise, her heart would burst from her chest. As for why she had taken off her clothes, it was because that's what they did on TV. After the kiss, or after he had fed her green tea, did it not follow that they were supposed to . . .

But he hadn't taken off her clothes, so she had to do it by herself. She wasn't sure exactly what was supposed to happen. It's just that everything that followed was always censored from the screen, and Xia Ling didn't know what to do.

He stayed with her in silence and didn't even warm her two pitiful white lotus-like lips.

"It's cold, don't catch a cold, put them back on." He draped her clothes over her shoulders, got up and walked to the window, lit a cigarette again and casually turned on the lamp on the table. "You stay here tonight. Tomorrow morning there is breakfast on the second floor. You can use anything in the room as you like. I will leave first. If there is anything, call me."

"No, don't!" Xia Ling hugged him, barefoot from behind, and said softly, "I'm sorry, I was not well behaved. I shouldn't, never again. I just love you a little bit, I don't know why. If you leave, what's the point of me being here alone? Don't leave me, please. Take me home. I want to go home."

The back of Yue Qianshan's shirt was wet with tears.

On the way home, Mrs. Yue called on the phone two or three times.

Xia Ling slowly calmed down, feeling lucky for no reason, although she couldn't think clearly about many things.

"Thank you for today. Can you leave me your number?" Before getting out of the car, Xia Ling was already sober for the most part.

Why had Yue Qianshan put her clothes back on that night? Xia Ling couldn't understand it. Later, she asked the salesgirls who worked with her. They all said, "A man can't wait to take off your clothes. To put clothes on you, it must be because he is a responsible man and he values you." Was that the reason? As if a flower had blossomed in Xia Ling's heart, she could not help but laugh as she walked lost in her thoughts.

"Are you busy tonight?" Xia Ling's cellphone shook. Autumn Rain had sent her a message.

"Yes, I have a date."

"With a man, right? He hasn't arrived yet?"

"Not yet. He is late but he will come," Xia Ling replied, typing each letter laboriously. Tears quietly filled her eyes, and she couldn't see the screen. If she really had faith in him, where did the heartache come from? After typing, when she was just about to press send, she hesitated and deleted the message. She typed only three words: "He will come."

"It's such a cold day. Don't wait, go home."

"No."

As if. As if by waiting a little longer, she could will his car into being in front of her.

"This man is really not a person of substance. He has made you wait so long. He is not that important."

Of course he was important, otherwise why would she have waited for so many years? From the beginning of youth to the twilight of youth.

"This was our agreement twenty years ago."

"Agreement? How do you know it's not a joke?"

Was it? Yue Qianshan, is this really the case? If so, was everything you gave me all a joke?

All the emails, the text messages, the phone calls and all the gentleness and love that you have given me in the depths of my memory. In fact, you didn't have to be like this. As the general manager of a five-star hotel, why would you be so warm and accepting to a wine salesgirl? No matter if I accidentally spilled wine on you, or served the wrong fruit tray by mistake, you were always gentle. There was never any accusation, no harshness, and even when the boss criticized me, you tried to smooth things over by laughing it off. Look at our call records, the longest was two hours, thirteen minutes and forty-five seconds. Not to mention those nights that belonged to us. Those lonely nights of burning desire, which only burned more fiercely because of your arrival. What were those?

The longing she had for Yue Qianshan after that drunken night was still so fresh. In the days after – how much she had wanted to see him again. She would lead others to his usual seat so that, when he did come, she could have an excuse to seat him in the small card room on the second floor. That way she could spend a few trembling minutes alone with him while she poured him a glass of whisky. Was that a lot to ask? Of course not. This was the most she could do to control herself, control her longing and go on living. How many times had she fantasized kissing him, biting him on the shoulder, holding him for a long time, not letting go? She could give up all these ideas, as long as she could keep seeing him, in the noisiest and densest night of this city, if she could just keep seeing him.

The frequency of Yue Qianshan's visits to the nightclub did not change much from before. Most times he brought groups of friends. In front of those people, he often sat lost in his thoughts, the most distant guest. She, in turn, was the quietest liquor sales-girl. She suppressed her frantic heartbeat, doing her best to spew endearing terms to her customers and promote her liquor with smiles on her face. She didn't dare look at him, for fear that he would see into her mind. As a result, her heart was like a piece of paper that had been repeatedly crumpled and unfolded, sup-pressed, happy and covered with scars.

One day, she couldn't help it anymore and wanted to talk to him about her feelings. She called him.

"My birthday is coming soon, can you spend it with me?"

6

Waiting.

Xia Ling was born in early summer. Today, in a white cotton dress, she looked like a lotus root, or like a table lamp in the dark at the head of the bed, radiating a fascinating light around her. In front of her was a cup of rose petal tea. Her long hair danced playfully in the wind. Her skin had a dab of powder, smooth and tender. She was beautiful sitting in the crisp and bright sunlight. How pleasant it was, in such bright weather, sitting in front of the window of a restaurant filled with the aroma of grilled steak.

Yue Qianshan promised to come and be with her for dinner, although he hadn't shown up yet. Xia Ling didn't want to rush him. Seeing the traffic rolling outside, she was willing to wait quietly.

It turned out that waiting for the one you love was so sweet.

Xia Ling couldn't help laughing.

Looking up, she caught sight of a familiar figure riding a KFC food delivery bicycle. The cyclist rode wildly through the crowd, attracting the glares of all the passersby. Even though the face only flashed by Xia Ling thought, *It's her, it must be!*

Xia Ling hurried forward a few steps, shouting hoarsely in the direction of the cyclist, "Little Jing! Jing!" But the cyclist was nowhere to be seen. Xia Ling stood at the entrance, on the sidewalk, on the tips of her feet, looking off into the distance, unwilling to give up. She just wanted to ask if Jing had seen her pager.

"Next time you don't need to stand out here to welcome me," a masculine voice said.

Yue Qianshan had just arrived and was smiling at Xia Ling. Today Yue Qianshan wore a white half-sleeved shirt and a pair of dark blue trousers, with a Hermès belt around his waist.

"Welcome you?" Xia Ling gave Yue Qianshan an insolent look. "I saw a friend of mine just now. She might have stolen my pager."

"So you want to grab her and torture her before sending her off to the police station?"

"That's not . . ." Xia Ling was dumbfounded by his question. "I just want to ask her about it."

"Ask what? You just said 'probably.' So there's no proof. Even if you had evidence, there's not much you could do. Buy another one; it's not a big deal," Yue Qianshan said, as he walked into the restaurant, patting Xia Ling on the back lightly.

Xia Ling looked at him sharply and shook his hand off her shoulder. "What do you know? Many things are not as simple as you think. You have money, and you think a pager that costs one or two thousand yuan is nothing. But what about other people who aren't as well off? Do you know how many smiles, how many exhausting words, how many glasses of wine we have to drink before we earn this handful of money? Rent, water and electricity, meals, cosmetics, shoes, clothes, purses, sanitary napkins – what doesn't cost money? Not to mention my brothers' tuition, my dad's medicine, my mother's muscle strain. Mother is too thrifty even to buy a medicinal patch for herself . . . Do you know how long I had to save to get that pager? How big a deal it is? Sorry, I think it's a big deal!"

"It's your birthday today, be happy." Yue Qianshan glanced at her hopeless expression and hugged her shoulders.

"Not happy," Xia Ling said stiffly, but her tone of voice had become softer.

After being seated, Yue Qianshan ordered two Australian steaks, two dishes of foie gras, a plate of salad, a creamy mushroom soup and two glasses of red wine. He comforted her while eating.

"She was riding a KFC food delivery bicycle. It would be easy to find her at a KFC store within five kilometres of this area. But, forgive me, I don't think you should do that. Isn't it good to leave her a way out? Let her have some leeway. Give her a little breathing space. You're right, making money is not easy, but some things are far more complicated and difficult than making money. You are still young now, and you will gradually understand . . . And, of course, if you want, I'll buy you a new pager." Yue Qianshan swallowed the last bite of steak. "After dinner, do you want to find a place to rest?"

Xia Ling liked listening to him very much. His voice was broad, deep, steady and quite charming. Even if he was lecturing her, it was comforting listening to his words. It's just that she was a little uncertain about what he meant by "rest." But as long as she was with him, whatever they did was fine.

After entering the hotel room, she felt like a small animal caught in a trap, pacing back and forth without escape. Part of her wanted to flee, but part of her also wanted to stay. Everything was under his control, but everything was different from what she had imagined. That moment came so fast, and she didn't have the slightest chance to change her mind. But time seemed to stretch endlessly – it was a sharp pain that pierced the bottom of her heart. Even in a room set at sixteen degrees, Xia Ling was still sweating out of pain. Yue Qianshan must have sensed her resistance, because he kissed her tenderly and whispered sweet words in her ear. Xia Ling remembered the one time Jing had dragged her to a ballroom dance. A man had taken her by the hand and swept her skilfully around the dance floor. The skirts, the long hair, the eyes and drunken laughter. She was a savvy dancer, swaying along with the push and pull of her male companion. Yes, that time she danced freely, relaxed and cheerful.

"No matter how powerful the man is, at the end he always surrenders to the ladies." Yue Qianshan rolled over in bed. He lit a cigarette, almost out of habit. Xia Ling slowly gathered her memories, retracing her life, until she found reality. Bit by bit, her senses came back, and she struggled to get up. Just then a plum blossom fell softly onto the white bedsheets.

Yue Qianshan glanced down at it wordlessly. He sat contemplating it, smoking patiently, but with a frown. Xia Ling's body tingled with embarrassment and confusion. She bit her lower lip, unable to speak. *Need I explain? How should I explain? Will it put him under pressure? Does he think I will cling to him? Actually, I only wanted to do it once with him. I just wanted to do it once. Once is enough. Don't worry, I don't want anything, I love you and won't put you in a difficult position . . .*

Just as Xia Ling was plucking up the courage to say what was hidden in her heart, Yue Qianshan grabbed her firmly by the shoulders, and pressed her to his chest. "I thought you girls in the karaoke bar were quite casual . . ."

There was nothing to explain. Everything had long been concluded. Her nose suddenly sore, she stood up and said, "I'm sorry. My period is ahead of schedule. I will go to the bathroom."

In the bathroom, she shook like a leaf battered by the late autumn wind. Whether he knew that it was her first time was not important anymore. Even if she told him, he would question whether it was true. *It's better to be silent, whatever he thinks.*

When they came out of the hotel, he held her hand tightly, took her to the jewellery store and bought a diamond necklace: "For your twentieth birthday. From now on, no matter where you go, I will be with you."

Since that day, she never had real pleasure, no matter who she was with, no matter where she was. It's just because whenever she started having a good time, she would think of Yue Qianshan's words: *I thought that you girls in the karaoke bar were quite casual.* Tears would flow down, just like that, and her heart became cold, very cold, and all hope was crushed into despair.

7

That necklace was Xia Ling's first piece of jewellery in her life, and she cherished it so much. The other salesgirls were sharp-eyed, and when they saw it, they all touched and praised it. "The necklace is not bad. How much did it cost? You're too modest. Buy a larger one. This kind of fake diamond is for glamour, and you should get another one as big as it comes. The best one is the kind that can blind someone as soon as they enter the door." Every time she heard these words, Xia Ling pursed her lips and smiled, gently retracting the pendant from their hands and stuffing it back into her clothes, but she felt uneasy in her heart.

There are layers of unbreakable prejudice in this world. As an example, people working in nightclubs must be casual with sex.

Example: girls from poor families must wear artificial jewellery.

Example: Xia Ling's love for Yue Qianshan must be for money.

These prejudices always made Xia Ling unhappy, but she didn't want to defend herself. What was the point? You can't explain it to every person. The best answer was to try hard to turn one's own situation around.

Summer was particularly pleasant. Just like a cicada, hiding in the shade of the branches and screaming its heart out all summer. After the flowers in the wild apple forest wilt and die, the green and acidic fruits grow first into a bean, a date, then a fist. With time, they grow bigger and bigger, and the fragrance becomes more alluring. Xia Ling's figure also grew fuller and curvier. Often a fleeting sensualness touched the corners of her eyes, like thin snowflakes that melt in the palm of a hand, never staying for long, and can only be remembered.

People around her felt that Xia Ling had changed, but they couldn't figure out exactly where or how she had changed. She seemed perpetually busy, always leaving in a hurry after work. Some girls invited her to go shopping, but she never had any free time. Sometimes she said she was doing her hair, another time she said she was eating with friends and yet another time she had to help someone move something or other. In short, her whereabouts and activities were unknown. On several occasions, she went to work carrying a heavy cloth bag and hung it on the wall. One of her coworkers finally couldn't restrain her curiosity, and rifled through it. It turned out to be books borrowed from the Provincial Library: *Cultural Journey, Across America, Introduction to Office Tutorial, First Intimate Contact, Social Etiquette, The Road to the Future* and an adult college entrance examination form.

"Xia Ling, do you plan to take the adult college entrance examination? What's the use of taking this? Look at how many genuine college students have no jobs. The country doesn't save job spots for them anymore, so they have to look for jobs by themselves. You're an adult with a college diploma competing with them. Isn't that like an egg hitting a stone? Do you know how we're different from them? We have the opportunity to make big money every day. Look at all the girls who run off with big shots. How many sisters have done that? Yanzi, Sister Bai, Qingqing? They all hooked up with rich guys and don't have to work here anymore. Those college graduates who want to find big money can't find it as easy as us. With your skills, you can tell who's rich at a glance. So just dazzle them with your beauty. Isn't that easier than learning English? We have to use what we know, right?"

The bar had just opened, and there were no guests yet. Her coworker sat on the long wooden bench in the change room and fiddled with the books disdainfully, chatting with Xia Ling.

"But those girls, how many of them are married properly?" Xia Ling challenged.

"What marriage are you talking about? When you are being taken care of, what's the point of talking about feelings? Who's dumb enough not to take advantage of being young and pretty to get some money in the bank? After, you're free to open a hair salon, a clothing store, and if you want, find an honest guy to marry. Do you think the wives of the men who come in here are thrifty? Aren't they all older women who are out of shape, who are happy to let you steal their husbands? Besides, if you really catch one of those awful men, the one who marries you must be so unconscionable that he can dump his wife any day of the week. So that means tomorrow he'll probably dump you as well. So, tell me, who isn't young and beautiful for a few years? There are plenty of girls more beautiful than you. Even if you're married, can you hold on to your man? The bottom line is, don't think so much, just grab as much money as you can. We don't have a diploma or good education. After a few years, what kind of work can we find?" The coworker stuffed the books back into the big bag again, folding and creasing the corners of the book covers.

"That's why I want to get a diploma." Xia Ling took out the books again and smoothed out the covers.

"Well, you don't listen. When you finish studying, you'll be an old maid, and by then it'll be too late to save you. Your youth will be gone, and you'll have a piece of useless paper. You'll regret it then."

Xia Ling's contacts with Yue Qianshan were Zenlike. "Come and go" as he liked, no demands, no requests. He had a family, a son and so many brothers. As for her, she seemed to be the redundant one. Often, late at night, Xia Ling would ask herself if she had been too shameless to give her first time to such an immoral man so easily. She soon figured out the answer to this question. She loved him, so she took their relationship seriously. That was all there was to it. *What a blessing to be able to give my first time to the one I love.* Whenever she thought of this, Xia Ling laughed inwardly. She could smell the rush of adrenalin and the sweat on his body again. In the end, she believed that that drop of blood that had stained the bedsheet wasn't the measure of their relationship. Love was.

She often fell asleep with a book in her arms. When she woke up, the lamp was still on.

On this day, Xia Ling went to bed late again. She was still dreaming, but was awakened by the ringtone of her pager:

"Girl, are you free tonight? – Yue Qianshan"

She shook herself awake, put on her clothes and ran to the canteen where there was a phone, at the entrance of the alley, to return the call.

"I'm going to work tonight, but I can make time."

"Don't go, stay with me." He hung up without waiting for her to agree.

Xia Ling faintly knew that something was wrong. In the past, he would take her out; after, he would drive her back to work when the time came. Her instinct was right. That night, Yue Qianshan was unable to free his mind from worry. Sweat densely packed his forehead, and there was an inexplicable anxiety in his eyes. This anxiety was like a snake slithering out of a dry, moss-covered well, wrapping itself around her delicate body. Xia Ling was a little scared. But she wanted to help him resolve his dilemma. She said to him, "Let me help."

"Don't move!"

He pinched the back of her neck with one hand. She felt that her head was about to break in his hands. Her mind was grey, like her head was being plunged into a deep pool, unable to breathe, not knowing how deep the water was. Water was all around, no light, and nobody in her vision of darkness. Any struggle was futile, and Xia Ling could only drift with the current.

Finally, he let out a beastly growl. He buried his head in her chest for a long time. Silence took over the room.

He dropped on the bed, rolled over and looked hollowly at the ceiling with deadened eyes. Xia Ling moved closer to him and asked softly, "What's the matter?" He made no motion, no response.

She helped light a cigarette, brought it to his lips. He took a drag and exhaled, before pinching it out.

She lay gently on his chest. "Tell me what the woman you love is like." He closed his eyes, the expression on his face like a piece of soap thrown in the water, slowly softening and melting.

"Perfect hair, high heels. Knowledgeable, wise. Nice voice, fine skin." Xia Ling smiled as she listened.

"Big brother, shall we make a date twenty years from now?"

"Sure."

"On Valentine's Day, twenty years from today. On February 14, 2019, we will meet at the door of the Blues Bar. Do you dare?"

"Dare. As long as I am still around."

"Good, big brother. I know you'll be there."

That night, when Yue Qianshan took her back home, he held her for a moment. "Girl, if you have a chance, leave this city. The winter here is too cold and long, and it's depressing. Go to the south, where there's more sun. The weather is better, and you'll be happier."

8

Guests lined up at the door of Lonely Face Club. Inside was a big, noisy crowd. Xia Ling glanced inside. Judging from the crowd, it was about half past nine. The wind died down. Against the grey depths of the dark night, the sky showed a reddish colour, like a long-suppressed cry. Now it was not so cold, but gloomy clouds covered the sky.

"Hey, have you read the weather forecast? There will be snow tonight," one doorman said to the other.

Autumn Rain sent another message: "If you are near Chenyang Road, there is a Lonely Face bar. Go in for a drink. The weather is so cold. Put it on my account – the account number is 0228."

"No need."

Xia Ling's heart had been frozen. She responded mechanically, without anxiety or pain. She naturally knew that it would be futile to wait any longer. Sometimes you can clearly see the end, but you just don't want to admit it. On WeChat, for example, there were many poisonous articles. "There are no ugly women, only lazy women"; "Hold on a little longer, maybe you will discover a gold mine"; "If you don't work hard, you will never know how strong you are"; "If you don't lose weight, you will never know how beautiful you can be." On and on, these 'news' articles monotonously emphasizing the importance of putting in effort while ignoring the uncertainty of the result. If one could become more beautiful on one's own, why would medical beauty treatments be so popular after all these years? If persistence was rewarded, then all those young people who suffered sudden deaths after working '996' jobs – working a schedule from 9:00 a.m. to 9:00 p.m., six days a week – what did they get? Who said there must be a gold mine under your feet? Why wouldn't it be an abyss, waiting to swallow you whole? If the direction is right, perseverance will get twice the result with half the effort. If the direction is wrong, persistence is futile, like trying to get a fish from a tree.

Knowing that she would not see him tonight, she put away her phone. But to just leave like this? The twenty-year agreement was a joke after all. Looking inside, the DJ had already begun to spin her records. But Xia Ling could not hear the music. She tried her best to scan the face of every guest, trying to recognize the familiar face she wanted to see in the crowd.

This was the second time she'd waited for him like this. Like before, he hadn't shown up.

9

The first time he stood her up was after Xia Ling had quit her job at the Blues Bar.

Looking at the unruly crowd inside the club, Xia Ling was thankful she hadn't worked at the Blues Bar for too long. She had left before the summer of that year was over, the year she had met him. Yue Qianshan once painted a picture of her future, and she wanted to live in the way a woman he loved would. A woman like that would not be selling alcohol in a bar. She would be wearing power heels and a curvy skirt, walking in and out of shimmering office buildings. She would not be living in an unkempt brick shack with only one public toilet in a hutong; she would be living in a well-furnished high-end condo with a beautiful view of the river. She would not be commuting to work every day on a bicycle bought from a second-hand market. Instead, she would be driving her own red sports car, flaunting it through the streets. In short, selling wine at the Blues Bar wasn't compatible with the life of a woman that he could love. So Xia Ling decided to start a new life.

She ached to tell Yue Qianshan that she had quit her job at the bar and wanted to start her life over again. She wanted him to know all the things she planned to do to change her way of life.

But the same time, she had some bad news to tell him, something terrible. What that news was she could hardly admit to herself, but it was already growing inside her. If others found out, she would be shunned. It would cause such a scandal.

If they couldn't meet at the Blues Bar, where would they meet? It was as if Yue Qianshan was gone, like a soap bubble evaporated in the sun, no trace: no call, no text. The ground underneath Xia Ling disappeared; she seemed to be standing on air, her existence precarious and unstable. The only focus of her life had vanished.

The hotel. The hotel where he worked as the general manager – Xia Ling couldn't help but go there to look for him. At the front desk, the receptionist told her that Executive Yue was on a business trip and nobody knew when he would return.

That hotel was a place full of beautiful girls. Except for a slightly darker complexion and a mole on her chin, the receptionist was just as exquisite: her manners, smile and attire were perfect. "Then I will wait for him here, all right?" Xia Ling was helpless, almost begging.

"Sure, feel free to do what you want. But you are wasting your time. He really is on a business trip." The receptionist's smile was not warm at all, as if to politely compel whoever saw it to feel uncomfortable.

Xia Ling stubbornly waited on the sofa in the lobby, looking at the hotel guests come in and out. Perhaps it was the extravagance of the hotel around her, but an inkling, a feeling surfaced in Xia Ling's heart: Was it possible that this man was not even real? She had a trace of doubt about his existence. But there was something indisputable that proved he was a real person. It was not the diamond necklace on her neck, but what she carried inside herself everywhere she went.

10

A few days after that, Xia Ling left the city and went south just like he had told her to. In Guangzhou she opened an online shop. In her spare time, she studied hotel management. These were hard days, and she had little money.

Barely scraping by, she gave up the dream of having her own shop and ended up selling pancakes at a roadside stall. Around this time, she met a neighbour, Sister Xuan. Xuan had a hair salon and liked doing nails.

"Let me do yours," Xuan said.

"No, it'll only make my work harder."

Xia Ling's hands were rough and stiff, her nails a faint yellow-greenish colour. The yellow was from the pancake mix she spread out every day. The green stains were from chopping green onion.

"Why don't you find another job? Or get married to a man who doesn't dislike you? Why do you have to live such a hard life? Look at your growing belly. What will you do?"

"I'm okay, Sister Xuan; I will be fine after I finish university."

In the evenings she set up her food stall. People in the nightclub across the road came to buy night snacks. Seeing the nightclub goers, that familiar feeling came back to her. She had known that decadent life once, up north. The scent of cigarettes and cologne on a man. All that reminded her of Yue Qianshan.

She was so hard up for money, she hadn't sent any cash back to her family for a long time. Like usual, her family urged her to contribute her savings. In order to stop these "debt collection" messages, she turned off her pager. Three or four months after her exam was over, she turned it back on. She had more than thirty messages:

– Sis, please send money immediately. Father is hospitalized. Lung cancer has spread. - Second brother

– Sis, Third brother has come home. Please return. Father is not doing well. - Second brother

– Return now. Father in ICU. - Second brother

– Sis, Father out of danger for the time being. You must return quickly. - Second brother

– Lingzi, when will you be back? Your dad has been waiting for you, and he refuses to take his last breath. Come back quickly! - Mom

– Sis, Dad passed away. He wanted to see you. He said he hoped you are well. - Second brother

The last one was:

– Sister, I don't know if you still use this pager. Father owed more than 10,000 RMB in medical and funeral expenses. Mom and elder brother borrowed money from everywhere, and still need 2,500. If you have the money, call me. - Second brother

Xia Ling looked at the messages and cried bitterly. *Why did I turn off the pager? Why didn't I receive this news earlier?*

The man who loved her the most was gone.

From this point on, Xia Ling, you have no father. That father who held you on his shoulders since childhood and listened to the sound of crickets in the grass and went to work in the fields is gone. That father who watched your mother steam buns and hid two buns for you so that your brothers would not find them – that father is gone. That father who was picking the fruits on an apple tree, who saw you crying when you were scared by an old cow, who jumped down from the tree and hugged you – that father has left you! That father who coughed all night and couldn't sleep well, the one who took you on the train to the big city, and who asked you to go home and visit more, that father is no more.

Who would have expected that the day when your father wore a blue uniform to see you off from home was the last time father and daughter would be together? Do you regret it? Regret that you didn't take another look from the train window? Regret that you didn't write another letter to your home? Regret that you didn't go back to see him all these years? Xia Ling, how could you forget the hand that waved in mid-air to bid farewell to you?

11

Xia Ling did not go back home. Instead, she burned a sheet of joss paper and a handful of hell banknotes at the road intersection, and kowtowed facing north. The rolled-up, cindered papers under the cyan streetlamp were blown away by the midnight wind, blown upwards, like a flapping butterfly, floating high, unwilling to fall. She knew this was because her father refused to forgive her.

No matter how deep hate is it cannot cross the boundary between yin and yang. But if you hate this very boundary separating yin and yang, there's no escape.

She fell ill. Lying in a small hot room, she wanted to die. When her only friend, Sister Xuan, gently awakened her, Xia Ling squeezed out a smile. But tears burst out from her eyes, hot and bitter. Xuan hugged her and held out a bowl of chicken broth.

"Are you better? Let's go to the hospital if not. If you die, you leave behind the old and the young. How will they survive? Don't worry, just rest. I have money to care for you."

Xia Ling let tears drip down from her swollen eyelids, shaking her head weakly.

Xia Ling got better after that. What's more, Sister Xuan introduced her to a hotel manager, and Xia Ling got a job in the sales department of a three-star hotel. Like an unstoppable arrow shot into the sky, she was full of energy and enthusiasm. As part of her job, she put together a client list, organizing conferences and tourist groups. The hotel's occupancy rate broke new records and she was promoted to sales manager. After another year, she became assistant general manager.

All this success seemed to come from out of nowhere, as if someone far away was helping her.

Later, a new five-star hotel needed an assistant general manager. As it turned out, the hotel contacted Xia Ling and offered her the position. She was a success. With so many connections, she even arranged a job for her brother.

No longer worried about being poor, Xia Ling missed Yue Qianshan more than ever.

After work one day, she turned off the office lights. She dialed the familiar number, one digit at a time. When she finished dialing, she held her breath and waited for the sound of his voice. The silence was broken by harsh sound: "Sorry, the number you dialed is not in use."

Just like when she had turned off her pager, the only clue he'd left her was also broken. Unwilling to give up, she searched for him on Baidu. As it turned out, she uncovered several pieces of news. There was an article describing how Mr. Yue, a prominent hotel manager, had been caught up in an investigation into government corruption in H City. Xia Ling noted the date, which coincided with the dates around when she had last seen him – when he had told her to go south. Could it be that he had tried to protect her? After all, that kind of government investigation knew no bounds. It would have dragged everyone down, including her.

The news report went on: While the government officials implicated had been disciplined, Mr. Yue had been exonerated. Still, because of the investigation, Mr. Yue had lost his wife, his family. Xia Ling desperately searched for more, and discovered that he had started out his life again, just like her, and had become a successful businessman. But anything more than that, she could not find.

"So that's it."

The stone that had weighed on Xia Ling's heart for more than ten years broke apart in an instant. The entangled hurt she thought she could not forgive all her life dissipated so easily. Moonlight poured into the room like smooth silk. On Xia Ling's soft and delicate skin, a pair of white and translucent pearls hung from her ears, bathed in the moonlight, lonely and lovely.

Why didn't you tell me what happened earlier? I've hated you for so many years, and it's all for nothing? Where are you?

12

Xia Ling raised her wrist to check the time – it was almost ten o'clock.

A half-drunken man came out talking on the phone. He had on a worn leather jacket, a hat and a scarf around his neck. Only half his face was exposed. His voice was so low she couldn't hear the content of the conversation. She only saw him looking back at the bar's street number, probably telling the other party the name of the bar, and then tapping on the phone a few times. With nothing else to do, Xia Ling speculated. He might be sending his location to whoever he was talking to.

Xia Ling was only too familiar with this situation. The performance inside had already begun, and the men and women spending the night had waited for this moment – cigarettes, wine, dice, swinging, all went into this ball of noise. If you wanted to make a phone call, you had to go to the bathroom or outside.

"Hey, do you have a cigarette? I could use one," Xia Ling smiled and said to the man wearing the scarf next to her.

The man looked at her, pushed his scarf up, took a step away and retrieved a box of Harbin smokes with his right hand. He flicked his index finger toward the bottom of the cigarette box, and a cigarette popped out.

Xia Ling pinched it with two fingers, and the man retracted the cigarette case, took out a lighter and lit it, leaning close to Xia Ling's lips.

In the flame, Xia Ling's lipstick was dazzlingly beautiful, her long curly hair gleamed with crimson shimmer, her thick eyelashes like the wings of a butterfly in early summer and her skin smooth and delicate, sending ripples through one's heart just like twenty years ago.

Xia Ling took a deep drag on the cigarette, looked up and said, "Thank you."

At the same instant, the flame went out. A Toyota came to a stop by the side of the road, driven by a beautiful middle-aged woman. The man turned his head and glanced at Xia Ling, his gaze like candlelight swayed by the wind, the slight flutter making one's heart tremble. Xia Ling didn't want to meet his eyes. There were some people she could look at, and there were some she could take into her heart. But there were some, they could only light a cigarette for her. Xia Ling turned her face away.

The man got into the car alone, disappearing like frost after a snowfall.

"Hey, sir, please don't go yet!" The bar door swung open and out ran a girl in staff uniform with a childish face and crude makeup that did not conceal her beautiful features, chasing after him. The Toyota had already left.

"What's the matter?" the doorman asked.

"He hasn't settled the bill yet, it's whisky. If it's beer we could forget it, but whisky is so expensive!" The girl was anxious to the point of crying.

"Don't worry, you're a new employee and you don't know him. He is an old customer, and he uses his account every time. Account number 0228, you just need to enter the charge into the account for him." The doorman's voice was low and gentle, softly coaxing.

Number 0228, what a coincidence! Xia Ling raised her phone and glanced at WeChat again. *That's right, Autumn Rain's account number is 0228.*

Xia Ling took another deep drag of the cigarette, and exhaled smoke into the sky full of falling snow. The cold streetlamp, shrouded in a halo of crystal light, with its lampshade seemingly floating, was as distant as her fading memory. She couldn't help chuckling. The mysterious man had been watching her in secret all along.

Her phone vibrated again, and it was Autumn Rain's message: "Girl, go in for a drink, the winter here is too cold and too long, long enough to suffocate anyone . . ."

Time just stopped. Snow fell on her ears, like bamboo leaves stroking the window bars, making a "sha . . . sha . . . sha" rustling sound. Xia Ling closed her eyes, not knowing when the cigarette in her hand had dropped to the ground. Her mind went blank.

In the ripples of her heart, it was that wintry night when they first met, that burly figure, the thick voice, his whole body emitting brilliance that could not be obscured by anyone. Autumn Rain, divorced, No. 0228, smoking man, whisky, remarried to the beautiful woman in a Toyota, Yue Qianshan . . . For a long time, she tried her best to search for connections. But in her memory, nothing but sighs came up again and again, broken up like starlight on the ground.

This was a fact. He had left before she was finished waiting for him.

She burst into tears, brought her lips close to the phone and left a message: "Tell me, that winter night, why did you let me go?"

After a long, long time, a line of words flashed: "Girl, I have never been a gentleman, but I don't prey on others."

"Then, have you ever loved me?"

This question. This question that she pondered over and over for the last twenty years, this question that she had always wanted to ask but never dared. This question that she could not bring herself to ask, not until today, today, no, not until this moment, when she finally asked it. But the answer was an automatic reply:

– Autumn Rain has turned on friend verification, you are not his (her) friend yet . . .

In the distant and quiet sky, a faint rosy colour interlaced with the dazzling neon lights, white snow fell, flake upon flake. Xia Ling raised her face to greet these delicate visitors from the sky.

They were so pure and happy, dancing and jumping, embracing the world without worries.

The noise at Lonely Face gradually quieted down. An Eason song was playing gently in the flickering candlelight:

> I came to your city and walked the path you walked
> Imagining how lonely you were without me
> Holding the photo you gave me, the familiar street
> It's just that, without you, we will not return to that day
>
> Will you suddenly appear
> At the coffee shop on the corner
> I will wave a greeting with a smiling face
> Sitting and chatting with you
>
> How I want to see you
> Look at your recent changes
> Not talking about the past
> Just a greeting
> Say something to you
> Just a few words
> Haven't seen you for a long time . . .

Xia Ling stopped walking, a gentle expression on her face. A smile flickered across her eyes.

"He is nineteen years old, not a child anymore," she said to her secretary, over her phone. "Next time, don't pick him up. Let him go home by himself."

"Yes, ma'am."

The sun shone above. The diamond on Xia Ling's neck shimmered.

Far up north, in H City, the sky was overcast with dark clouds. A man smoked a cigarette at his desk, watching a jackdaw on a branch outside the window.

The door opened. A female assistant poked her head in. "Mr. Yue, should we send the wire transfer now to Xia Ling, just like last time?"

Yue Qianshan waved his hand.

"Okay, sir, I'll do it right away. She'll appreciate the capital investments you've made into the Xia Ling Hotel Group. Are you sure you don't want me to tell her you're the angel investor who's backed her all these years?"

Yue Qianshan motioned the assistant not to say any more. He pointed to the crow on the branch outside the window. The assistant turned to look, but the crow fluttered its wings and flew away.

The crow's cries were as dry and rough as a mottled wall in the sun's glare. The branches swayed in the cold wind, and just then a twig turned green.

Maybe spring is coming . . .

Canadian

Moonlight
in the Palm of My Hand

Ellen Chang-Richardson

I HELD DEATH FOR THE FIRST TIME WHEN I WAS ELEVEN.
It might have been a Wednesday. It might have been summer. It
might have been if only I could really remember. Up until that
moment, death had been nothing more than a distant thought –
borne up on a black brush stroke or wrapped in the triumph of a
Disney movie.

An animated villain.

A leaf on a passing tree.

Yueliang had come into my life hopping. Across a banquet hall
table, under the loops and swirls of calligraphic ink. Horsehair and
bamboo brush smooth and stiff under my fingertips as I painted
scenes of peonies and tea leaves and golden koi fish. Adventurous,
button nose–first, this white little fluff had made herself known.
To me, she echoed the crescent shapes strung along the walls. *Mid-
Autumn Moon Festival at the Four Seasons Villa.*

I had had Yue for what felt like only a few days, though if I look at a calendar and parse it rationally, I probably knew her for closer to seven or eight months. I feel like by the time I held her cold little body in my hands, the air was thick enough to mark a difference.

You see, Yue and I would often visit the park in the middle of the housing compound. A friend might join us, depending on the day, depending on our mutual mood. Often, Yue would sit in my lap and nibble away on some strips of hay I would think to pack in my pocket from home.

Other times, she would bounce across the blanket I lay down on the grass as I read the newest additions to my small but growing library. This day, however.

Yueliang was as white and as cold as her namesake.

As I knelt over her hard little body, I stared down, unable to shed a tear. An incessant whirring had picked up in the space behind my ears and tendrils of my light brown hair fell into my eyes. It was a stasis that would repeat itself seven years later at my maternal grandmother's funeral. The world had stopped. Reality, slow, as I thought back to the afternoon before.

We'd been out on the soft green grass, the two of us. We'd sat over there: by the man-made pond in the man-made park in our man-made compound. Yue had hopped in and out of my palm. Then up and over my arm. Fluffy and light, she had bounced around, green twists of grass caught in her small active mouth.

Green twists of grass.

I dropped Yue's body and ran as fast as my short legs could take me. Through the back gate, down the street, around the corner with that random birch tree and through the park hedges, back to the same spot I had sat the afternoon before. A new afternoon's sun beat down upon my head. Its warmth, a ghost, as I peered around me. Brackish pond, lined with algae and duckweed. Yellowing grass, swaying in the warm breeze. Swing set. Trees. Pebbles, crumbling underfoot. And the sign:

请勿进入草坪!

qǐngwù jìnrù cǎopíng!

Please keep off lawn!

Well, okay. I had seen that yesterday . . . but me, a budding rebel, had paid it no heed. Yue and I had plopped down on the grass. Yue, excited to simply get out of her cage; me, excited to dive into the book I had brought along. I had forgotten my blanket, but I'd figured it'd be okay as long as I kept a solid eye on her. With Yue's velvety ears twirling around my fingers, I spent the afternoon nose-deep in a treasured childhood story –

We all have those stories – the ones that punch us deep. No matter how many years pass us, this one continues to be mine. *In the midst of a separation* [my parents were beginning to fall apart too] *the parents of a twelve-year-old girl send her away for the summer, from downtown Toronto* [my hometown!] *to the childhood cottage of her mother's family in Alberta. Awkward and uncomfortable* [she wasn't alone] *among cousins she barely knew, the girl is left to her own devices* [what's new?]. *She wanders around without purpose – this place her own mother used to spend each childhood summer – until she discovers a heavy old-fashioned pocket watch hidden under the loose wooden floorboards of the small, dusty boathouse* [ah, antiques]. *Winding up the watch, the girl opens the boathouse's screen door into a different era. She haunts the footsteps of her twelve-year-old mother day after day, hour after hour, only to return to her own time and realize that no time had passed at all.* The book was a handful of comfort. It was something solid. To this day it still makes me wonder . . . if you stop long enough to count the spaces, how many threads could there be, dimensionally, between this moment and the ones that exist around it?

Snapped out of my thoughts, I looked a bit closer at the vista surrounding me. *Not much else here . . . what could have possibly happened?* A warm breeze picked up. A flutter of beige caught the corner of my eye. I looked again.

To the left of the main sign, there was another. A small, temporary fixture:

警告: 农药喷上
jǐng gào: nóng yào pēn shàng
Warning: Pesticides Sprayed

Yueliang was both my first, and my last, pet.

It's hard to trust yourself with another once you accidentally kill the first one ever placed in your care.

I could not return to her.

To this day, I have no idea who decided it was time to take care of her body, or when and how Yueliang was laid to rest. Was she placed in a swath of cloth and buried by the bushes? Or was she ditched by A-yi into that evening's trash? I will never know. Perhaps if I had had more peace of mind or perhaps if I were older, I would have been able to give Yue a proper ceremony. Be that as it may, I'd probably still have to ponder . . . *does one host ceremonies for negligence?* Whatever came to be, I could not return to her.

Some days, there are breaths of time where I allow myself the space to venture back. When that happens, I can feel her again, beneath my fingertips. Her soft ears, still and silent. Her half-closed eyes, hazy orbs of sandblast once inquisitive and bright. Her nose a slight, pale hue. It's strange how death manifests.

Before that day, death was something to be in awe of. It was pomp and circumstance. It was rippling white fabric. It was Buddhist ministrations on hot and humid hazy afternoons. Death was ritual. Death was a wide-eyed girl. Death was maybe, if one was lucky, a passage between this plateau and the misty corners of reincarnation. It's strange how it manifests.

For some, it's in the bones picked from the ashes of a cremation.
For others, in a tree that grows from a coffin the shape and texture of a seed.
For Yue, it was through her belly.

Once round and soft and warm, it exists forever cold and hard inside me, swollen by the chemicals that did not belong.

Coal Flowers
Isabella Wang

THE FIRE WASN'T THE ONLY THING I REMEMBERED from last night. Its flares lit up like an orange apparition, making me think for a second that I was dead, witnessing an explosion from inside the girths of a coal mine. There was also the absence of things I remembered for thirty-seven minutes, the time it took for the city to send rescue when respondent rates should have been much faster.

My parents migrated with me to this part of the Wu Su Ming industrial district two years ago, one August, when the water level in Yei Yei's diesel engine well had risen by three inches, like me. We left a short time after they had come back to visit our village and help my grandparents pickle fennel. Prepare the last of our season's harvest for winter.

When I was younger and my parents left our village for the city yearly, they taught me that *zai jian* did not mean goodbye but a promise: *we'll see each other again.* When I whispered these words to my grandparents for the first time at thirteen, I knew that it would be months before I saw them again. I pinky promised Yei Yei that I'd call often, and not dress to brace the weathers of my new environment without recalling the *qi* that circulated the six tenors of wind and rainy Julys to our Shan Xi, surrounded by mountains.

Ma, Ba Ba and I located to the outskirts of Beijing, home to 1.6 million migrant workers and more of us who'd been turned away. Upon arriving to the big city on borrowed money from relatives, some are denied contract jobs. They have no fare to travel back home, and despite being homesick, have no other choice but to remain.

Mr. Fang's Jie Yong's Lucky Deer Hostel housed two dozen families like mine. We each occupied a double bunk bed and a single window looking out into the road's distance, into rows of hostel homes and two abandoned railway lines mosaicking a memory of this community's chugging, inaudible past. An opaque curtain partitioned every room in our hostel in two. Our curtain was coral red. It hung like a thin sliver of contracting muscle, adjoining the left and right chambers of the heart.

We were politely intimate with our neighbours. Their pulse, their conversations and quarrels flowed into our own bloodstreams and hopes for a steadier future. We accepted this family as our other half; shared with them our meals and received in return the old company uniforms that their son had outgrown, passed down to me.

Our families worked most weekday and weekend shifts together. In the mornings, we travelled as a group to one of three coal mining collieries a forty-five-minute walk away. Their work was opencast. Nearby, on a different quarry, my mother and I assisted on-site until my father and his crew emerged at the end of the day from the tunnel pits underground. The unevenly paved roads that supported the weight of our walking absorbed sound from kilometres away. If a mine exploded, we'd hear it. The dirt around us trembled. Sometimes, if we were at home, Ma and Ba Ba's porcelain teaware would move just a centimetre along the window ledge that the three of us also shared as a prayer and dining table, lit with chamomile incense.

Men are paid twice a week on Tuesdays and Saturdays. Women and children are paid once with the men on Saturdays. At the end of every week, Ba Ba sat and counted our earnings, setting aside a saving of thirty yuan. Then he'd give me six one-dollar bills to run to the Zhang couple's convenience store on the other side of the road to buy cigarettes, more incense and one Pepsi as a treat for each of us. Once a cigarette package was opened, I usually snuck a loosie or two for the boy on the other side of the curtain. The next day, while his parents washed up, I'd hand him the stolen goods hidden underneath a bowl of Ma's hot rice porridge.

Our district is well-equipped for incidents like last night. Firefighters are constantly getting called to assist on-site at the mine with what Mr. Hong, the maintenance superintendent, calls "tragic mishaps." The job is considered too dangerous for women and children under the age of fifteen, so only Ba Ba had sanction to descend into the pits. Ma and I cleaned the lunch and restroom facilities. Upon instruction, we drove trucks to receive equipment being delivered to the colliery and transport large allotments of coal and debris to a temporary reserve. The remains of the earth's deposits are being slowly emptied out, hauled away by barges along the coiling spine of the Yangtze River.

Women with husbands are tasked with another job, which is to remember the telephone numbers of the district office, the state office and the mine rescue station. This detail wasn't made explicit in Ma's contract agreement. But naturally, within contiguous proximity of the tunnels' blast radiuses, we are the first to report any accidents heard or witnessed nearby out of fear for the safety of our loved ones.

Once the workers are trapped, a team has only a short time until methane reaches toxic levels underground. Then rescue efforts must be abandoned. Due diligence is a countdown. Which is why, from across the street, I made the call using a dial phone in the Zhang couple's convenience store and expected the fire brigade to come relatively quickly. I expected to be reunited with both my parents, like the time we'd made the calls to the district commissioner's office, then rescue station, but our fear had turned out to be a false alarm. A few women working in the lunchroom had heard an airplane hovering low, and that was enough to send the rest of us into panic. Before long, everyone's beloved husbands, fathers, brothers and uncles emerged, confused by the sirens and empty body bags that had already been laid aside for them.

"*Hái zi*, stay with me," Mr. Zhang ordered. "You just stay here by the glass over there. Your Ma and Ba will be out soon."

But before long, the fire took over our side of the hostel. A single fire truck eventually came, but not until thirty-seven minutes later.

For such a small building, the fire was given an ample head start.

When they heard my voice on the other end and learned that the place I was calling about was a hostel, the city could have told the responders to wait ten minutes, not thirty, and our home would have still been unsalvageable.

The city let the fire take our home away. Mr. Fang. My parents. Our neighbours who were our other half, and their son, the only friend I'd made since leaving my hometown.

The little Nokia flip phone we kept in a drawer was gone. I had no way to contact Nai Nai and Yei Yei, still waiting in Shan Xi for our phone calls to come.

At dark, the Zhangs didn't charge me for the Pepsi I drank before going to bed. They locked up the cash register and made room for me behind the counter, let me sleep there on the floor with Mr. Zhang's heavy coat and a stack of folded-up cardboards I used as a pillow. There was little I could do for the Zhangs in the store that they couldn't already do themselves. My plan was to go back to work the next day and ask around, see if there was space in a neighbouring hostel where I could stay.

During my first year in Wu Su Ming, the sound of quarry explosions unsettled me whenever I felt a pulse of their vibrations invade the private sanctums of our walls. The job followed me like an intruder into my home, coercing its way forcefully here. The gradients from our black-and-white TV began to remind me of the dust from quarry trucks that dirtied my face. At night, when the inflammation in my eyes burned, I often dreamed of myself crying and wiping them with my sleeve, but I could no longer see Nai Nai and Yei Yei clearly.

Over time, I grew to prefer hearing the explosions at home, because that meant Ma and Ba Ba were at least with me. I could be spared the worrying that it was one of them caught underground between violent cross breezes spewing ash and methane gas.

In my mouth, *kuàng*, the Chinese word for "mine," is only a tone different than *kúang*, meaning "mad" or "violent." There was a lot about our former situation that drove my parents mad: our income; the conditions of our work site; the uneasy energies of our "other half" on the other side of the curtain about these same grievances, whenever they upset the balance of Ma's lit incense during her spiritual hour. Other times, their anger was directed at me. I provoked them by wanting to go back to my grandparents in Shan Xi, or complaining about not being able to sleep more on a Saturday.

But even when Ma and Ba Ba were mad, they were not violent.

Ba Ba said that *kuàng* is *ji rou ji yi*. A muscle memory of the heart. "The earth experiencing it has tried to forgive for too long. Like some people, after a while, all they remember is forgetting how not to fear, be calm again."

"What is *ji rou ji yi*?" I asked.

"Muscle memory?" He echoed and thought for a moment. "You've observed how, at the beginning of each week, Ba Ba and his other crew members have to gather in the meeting room? To practise our evacuation procedure?"

"Yes." I nod.

"We do it to be safe. That way, our muscles know how to respond when there is not enough time to think."

Their drills rotated every week between fire and explosions, floods, electrical hazards and falling materials. In theory, these routines were supposed to make the men faster, more organized and experienced in the case of a real accident. With time, I grew to understand that the real muscle they were strengthening was fear, week after week, so that faced with real danger, all the muscles in the body suspended immediately in fear. The women and children here have experienced it too.

Ma and Ba Ba knew that the environment on the coal mines wasn't suitable for a child. My time with them on the colliery was only supposed to be a temporary arrangement. For an industrial job, the mine paid well. They hoped that if we worked together, our family may be able to save up for a small apartment. The goal was to convince Nai Nai and Yei Yei to live in the city one day. Then, I'd have a chance of pursuing an informal education, and get a job working in retail, at a restaurant or textiles factory. Anything more suitable for a girl.

I told my parents, "*Bù*. Even then, I'd want to stay with you. The colliery might need my help." I tried reasoning with them that I was used to the work, that I didn't mind the dust, the hard conditions if it meant I could be near my family.

"*Sha hái zi*," they chimed in concert. *Stupid child.*

Ma said sadly, "Our family survived eating grassroots and tree bark. Just when we thought the unrest, the political massacres were over, we brought a child into the world and she is surrounded by a wasteland and good-for-nothing explosions. It's as if our ancestors from the Revolution have come to haunt us."

"The spirits have nothing to do with us," Ba Ba intercepted. "We picked this job. We set up these conditions for ourselves. Only children who grow up in the metropolitan core with English and Chinese language proficiencies and an expensive education can afford to pay their parents back by never leaving the family home. Their parents can dream of clinging on to their children forever, but not us. If you want to put our minds at ease, you must leave and come back only to visit. Then we'll know that you are doing well for yourself and have not forgotten us entirely."

In truth, I was afraid of leaving them. At least here, on the coal mines with Ma and Ba Ba, I had a sense of purpose. Without them, in this city of twenty-one million, uneducated, I realized that I would have much greater difficulties finding a path to fulfill by myself.

The next day, I returned to work with just two small reminders of the ones I loved. The six yuan Ba Ba had given me were still in my pocket. The old company uniform from our neighbour's son was the only pair of clothes I now owned.

The mine was its own silent reminder. I'd never spent as much time with my parents growing up as these past two years, working with them in the district. All my memories of them were formed here.

Mr. Zhang showed up to the store early to drop off some left-over breakfast. Mrs. Zhang had prepared you tiao and tang yuan. I had forgotten what sweet sesame paste tasted like. I asked him if I could borrow a pair of scissors. His kindness touched me. He spoke to me at eye level, in a way that felt like he understood my loss.

"The news anchor will probably be here to interview my wife and me," he said. "They'll probably want to get a shot of the debris before the city comes and cleans up the area."

"How long before –" I looked to the other side of the road.

"I don't know. The work will probably be quick. Not much left behind out there. A new hostel will be up by the end of this week, I'm guessing."

When I didn't say anything, Mr. Zhang continued. "When the reporter comes, do you want us to tell them about you?"

"No," I responded. "Mr. Hong, the maintenance supervisor, can't know. He has no use for a girl who can only bring him one-third of the work."

"He'll find out eventually. Your parents will be taken off payroll."

I looked at the scissors in my hand. "Ba Ba has taught me about his work, and I'm wearing a boy's uniform. I'm going to cut off my hair and apply for a boy's job."

Mr. Zhang gave me a worried look, but when I explained to him, he seemed to comprehend.

Ba Ba had trained inexperienced teenaged boys coming and seeking this job for the money. They must have heard from some-where that the coal mines paid decently, and probably had pressures from home. In the first year, they found the work to be torture. They couldn't even cry down in the tunnels because it was so dirty down there, and they'd develop conjunctivitis. Still, most of them risked their lives and stayed. What other choice did they have?

I told Mr. Zhang that it would still be easier if I worked as a boy, at least until the summer was over. I needed an income in order to eat and pay for a place to stay. Buy a new flip phone. Then I needed a way to get back to Nai Nai and Yei Yei, and still have some money remaining that will last them in the village for the rest of the year. The mountains aren't getting as much rain as previous decades. There are many droughts in the year. Nai Nai can't produce enough crops on her small tract of land, and the soil is all hardened and inhospitable for new seeds to grow.

"They won't survive in the village this way," I said. "They try. Nai Nai is stubborn in her strong-willed ways. But I can't let my elders get weak and sick, wondering where in this world I've gone."

Mr. Zhang asked me to come back that night for dinner. He knew that I wouldn't get paid until later in the week. "You can stay here this week and keep an eye out at the store at night. So my wife and I know you are doing okay."

His words cast a small embrace. Pulling the fog tightly over my shoulders, I wore my memories of Ma and Ba Ba walking along this bumpy dirt road like an additional jacket, making me feel less alone.

Shortly after 9:00 a.m., Mr. Hong pulled up in his army-green Jeep Wrangler at the bottom of the work site. The coal mine tunnelled deep into the belly of a small mountain, which over the years had become more levelled to look like a plateau. Even so, any farther up could only be reached by light-weighted machines with a strong, traction grip. Too heavy, and the roof of the mine risked collapsing and trapping any underground workers miles deep inside.

Mr. Hong didn't usually oversee our work on Sundays, but he made an exception this time. He had been notified of the deaths of a handful of his workers. For once, their casualties weren't his responsibility.

The men were already gathered in the meeting room when he arrived. They were counting their numbers. Reassigning tasks. They needed to wait for the bit of wind to die down before it was safe to resume their activities from the evening before, but the work would be more dangerous without Ba Ba and several other crew to spot each other.

I walked to the mouth of the mine shaft and waited for them there. I didn't want to interrupt their discussions. I also couldn't go to the facilities and join the other women because I had yet to get my face dirty, and they would easily recognize me. The girders of the railway track led a straight path into the tunnel's dark depths. The transportation carts sitting on top of them were red and rusted. From the entrance, I could only see so far into this cleft of the mountain that I was not sure what its walls, its muscles remembered. I thought Ba Ba was a good man. But in that moment, I realized that despite his stories, there was much about the way that his men talked about limestone and ventilation that were unfamiliar processes to me. I didn't know the extent of the impact Ba Ba had left. If I rode on one of these carts and descended into the coal heart of the mountain, would its muscles sense my coming as a repercussion of my father and flinch?

As the wind withdrew, the sky returned grey, stoic and motionless. I heard the footsteps of the men against the peated gravel: I stepped outside the shaft and made myself known. Mr. Hong seized me with his look. I began to explain that I needed a job. I heard he was short on men. And I was shielding myself from the wind.

"Next time don't stand under the mine shaft if there is wind," he said. "You are inexperienced if you don't know that."

I opened my mouth, but one of the other men looking my way started to shake his head. Would I have to recount a backstory? Were they going to believe the lie I had prepared?

Mr. Hong just asked me if I had any money. He was interested in the cheap labour that had just shown up on his work site, less so of where I came from. When I reached into my pockets and took out the six yuan Ba Ba had given me, he nodded, satisfied. "That will last you for three days to rent the proper footgear and a hard hat. The battery for the headlamp in the hat, you'll have to buy. On Thursday, you get paid a probation salary."

I looked at the men. Their faces were as expressionless and unreadable as the sky. Mr. Hong sent me home after that. My training started on Monday.

For six yuan, I had traded my material reminder of Ba Ba for the life he'd led for his family.

All day, construction and news crews circulated our area. Since becoming a mining town, this sector of Wu Su Ming didn't see the faces of many visitors like it used to anymore. News was usually coming to us through the small screen of our television. The cause of the fire was unspecified. There were too many flammable curtains, too many people cooking and lighting incense or cigarettes at once. The debris from the hostel was mostly cleared within a day, as fast as the fire that took it. All that remained of it was a small photograph on the third page of the day's newspaper. The Zhangs were in the photo, standing next to the burned-down rubble.

From the mine, I had acquired two small pieces of coal. I placed them into a shallow, glass bowl that I had borrowed from Mrs. Zhang, alongside a pinch of salt, some water, a drop of laundry detergent and blue food colouring from the store. The process of making coal flowers is well practised in coal mining families.

Ba Ba made them with me on the day of my fourteenth birthday, one year after I had been on the mines. Within a day, the coal we had set aside in salt and ammonia crystallized, transforming it into something beautiful. Ma put the coal flowers I had made next to her incense. She said they were perfect decorations for our windowsill.

My parents deserved much more. A proper burial with flowers and family in their ancestral hometown. But I could only give them coal. As I counted the number of blue crystals starting to appear in the bowl, I thought they looked quite a lot like snowflakes. I hoped this was enough to put to rest Ma and Ba Ba's souls.

Egg Tart, Deconstructed

Eddy Boudel Tan

INDIFFERENCE IS SOMETHING MICHELLE FEELS OFTEN without realizing it. "Feel" may be the wrong word, because it doesn't actually feel like anything. Rather, it's the absence of feeling, of caring.

Indifference is what she feels now, sitting across the table from a man she's spent the past three years curating a life with. He appears more vulnerable than usual beneath the moody lighting of the restaurant. His eyes are always unnaturally open, blinking far less than those of other people. Michelle used to find this lack of eyelid movement rather alarming – when they did close, they did so dramatically, for effect – but now she's grown used to everything about this man whom everyone seems to admire. Even the precision of his jawbone and disarming smile have a duller effect than before.

Her head nods along to the predictable rhythm of his words, but she's distracted by her indecision about the dish in front of her. Does it remind her more of a nest of earthworms, or a bundle of elastic bands? It certainly doesn't resemble the lo mein from her childhood: untidy piles of steaming noodles and fleshy pink prawns, rich with fat and salt, served on chipped ceramic plates with faded blue detailing. The noodles before her are anemic, unloved. Instead of a generous heap, they're swirled gracefully into a little volcano. *Three bites tops*, she thinks to herself. A single prawn, deveined and glistening, leans against one side above a smear of green sauce reminiscent of toxic waste.

Her attention is refocused not by a sudden noise but by the momentary absence of sound. The man is silent at the other end of the little table, looking at her as though waiting for something, eyes wide and unblinking beneath jet-black eyebrows.

"Hmm," she responds, nodding in agreement to whatever it is he'd said.

He sinks back into the velvet banquette, and Michelle notices for the first time that the plush fabric is the same colour as her lips and wine. The man is silent as they look at one another from their opposite ends of the table. Michelle knows he wouldn't accuse her of not listening, or any other shortcoming for that matter. His perception of her is too generous. He simply smiles as he slices into the steamed fish in front of him with a shiny knife. It's a palm-sized filet, its head and fins left off the plate unlike how it used to be served in this restaurant.

Michelle's hand hovers above the chopsticks beside her plate, which look more like weapons made of ivory than dining utensils, before choosing to pick up a polished fork instead. She twirls the noodles the way she'd learned from an old roommate, an Italian. She brings the fork to her mouth, careful not to slurp them noisily like her father would do.

The man begins to speak again. She nods along, watching his lips form elegant shapes as they emit sounds that go unheard. Her mother likes to talk about how he looks like a movie star from

Hong Kong. This always embarrasses Michelle, but her mother is right. That is what he looks like.

She's grateful when a waiter arrives holding a rectangular plate, which he places carefully in the centre of the table. "Egg tart, deconstructed," he proclaims. Michelle leans forward to inspect the strange dish. She's been eating egg tarts for as long as she can remember. The rich, buttery aroma would always transport her back to her childhood, racing her brother across the linoleum floor of their parents' bakery. They used to peer through the plastic case at rows of glossy buns and flaky pastries. Her brother preferred the white pouches of mochi filled with peanut and sugar – he called them snowballs – but she's always loved the tarts with the glistening yellow filling best. Unlike some other places, their mother never browned the custard.

The dish in front of Michelle, though, looks nothing like any variation of the treat she's ever seen. It doesn't have the same decadent scent. In fact, it doesn't seem to smell like anything at all. Pale yellow dollops have been piped in an erratic pattern across the plate. Rather than flakes of delicate pastry, little coins of what appears to be shortbread are placed alongside each custard swirl, some face down and others balanced on their edges. She senses an urge to wipe her hands across the plate, mash together the components into a ball of cookie and cream. But then something catches her eye.

In the middle of the plate, held upright in the centre of a shortbread coin, is a white-gold ring with a single cushion-cut diamond. Michelle simply stares at it for some time, trying to make sense of the ridiculous combination of edible and opulent. She would have continued to stare in silence, but the man intervenes.

"I've loved you since the day you walked into my life. Remember? Your first day in the office. I called you Miss, and you said you answer only to Michelle."

He's blinking more frequently than ever before, as though he's been saving them for this moment. She looks at him and feels blank, like there's nothing there and she's nobody. The only thought running through her mind is that it was the second day, not the first. They met on her second day in the office.

"The last three years have flown by so quickly," he goes on, "and there's so much more in store for us. When I think about my future, and I think about it often, I see you there beside me. There's no version in which you're not there."

He pauses, then leans forward and takes both her hands in his. She doesn't move.

"Michelle Choo," he says, stretching out that last word like he's blowing on a dandelion, "will you be my wife?"

She squeezes his hands as hard as she can, not knowing what else to do. Her lips part, but nothing comes out. The man's easy smile begins to falter, the corners of his mouth twitching as though he's posing for a photograph that's taking too long to snap.

Finally, her hands let go of his and retreat beneath the table. Her lips come together, and she looks down at the diamond before closing her eyes.

"I have to run to the ladies' room," she says a second later.

She shuffles out of the booth and marches down the carpeted aisle, unsure of where the washrooms are located. She passes hushed conversations and the gentle clinking of silverware, but the noises sound unbearably loud in her ears. The restaurant is a maze of dimly lit halls and tables tucked around hidden corners, nothing like the wide open space it used to be with unflattering fluorescent lights and vinyl-covered chairs. When the kitchen served food that was greasy but tasted glorious. Before it had imported wallpaper and social media cachet. She remembers how the previous owner used to send her home with a takeaway bowl of sweet red bean soup for her parents, back when she still lived with them.

Ambient music is playing from speakers in the washroom when she barrels through the door. Relieved that it's empty, she rushes into a stall and sits on the covered toilet seat. She doesn't understand why she's here, why she reacted the way she did. She loves him. He's good to her. She's lucky to have him. She's won the lottery.

You are so lucky.

All she hears is her mother's voice, intention stressed beneath the kind words.

We are so proud of you.

"I know, Mom," she whispers to the tiles on the floor.

She flushes the toilet just to hear its sound, using a square of toilet paper to protect her fingers from touching the lever, before taking slow steps toward the bank of sinks along the wall. The water is almost scalding as she washes her hands beneath the bronze faucet. One pump of soap, then another, and another. She wipes her hands with a towel from a stack beside the sink.

Her reflection stares back at her as she stands upright and straightens the front of her dress. It was a purchase she'd agonized over for days before pulling the trigger, worth half a month's rent.

What a pretty girl, her parents would always say. They'd comb her hair and straighten her second-hand clothes, ask her to smile more.

She smiles at her reflection, and she knows her parents were right. She's prettier when she smiles, and she's learned how to do it so that her eyes take part in the trick.

Her fingers reach for her face and pull at her cheeks until her lower eyelids are inside out, exposing the pink underneath. Her lips stretch out as wide as they can before twisting into an animal's snarl. She stares at the beast in the mirror, and she feels something like calm.

Her hands drop beside her at the sound of the door, and she's suddenly pretty again. A woman steps into the room and offers a polite smile. Michelle does the same.

The dining room feels darker as she makes her way back to the table. The man could be made of stone considering how still he is, except for his left leg, which shakes like he's playing a kick drum. He watches silently as Michelle slides onto the velvet banquette.

"Yes," she says.

"Excuse me?"

"My answer is yes."

His face remains unmoved for a moment, uncomprehending, before his eyes crinkle and his teeth appear between upturned lips. His whole body shakes as he reaches across the table and takes her by the hand. He calls out to the waiter to bring the champagne, not noticing how limp her hand feels, not seeing the indifference in her eyes.

Fault Lines

Yilin Wang

DAI YING AND THE "BOYFRIEND" SHE RENTED FOR FOUR hundred yuán per day lingered near the entrance of an ancient quadrangle courtyard in Yibin, where her grandma, Nai Nai, still lived. Outside the courtyard gates, scarlet lanterns and crimson banners with calligraphy dangled. They always appeared around New Year's to summon good fortune, but never brought any luck to Dai Ying. Inside, Nai Nai must be counting the minutes until she and Cheng arrived, so they could all share the family reunion dinner. Finally, Nai Nai would stop chiding her for being single.

She turned to Cheng. "Are you ready?" He was dressed impeccably, his shirt buttoned to the top, his tuxedo pants ironed and straight. But he was only her old high school classmate, a partner in crime.

"Don't worry," he said. "I've got plenty of experience with visiting in-laws. Follow my plan."

"I know Nai Nai better than you."

"If not for me, you'd have had to hire that college kid or some forty-year-old creep who wants to date you. You need my help. You're a damsel in distress."

"And you're my employee." Dai Ying rolled her eyes. Other girls might fawn over a guy like him, well-dressed and eager to help, swooping in to save her like a warrior in a martial arts novel. But she chose him only because he was an old acquaintance, more trustworthy than a stranger.

She squeezed Cheng's palms with her sweaty hand. Two years ago, she would sneer at people who hired a fake date. But then she turned twenty-seven last year and as soon as she reached that age, Nai Nai began to call her a 剩女, a Leftover Woman. Then Baba passed away. Nai Nai scoured the city for matchmakers, ordered her to attend dozens of blind dates and dragged her to visit marriage markets. How could she bear to date, however, with Baba gone for less than a year, his body still unrecovered, unable to be buried and put to rest? "Do you want to be alone like your father?" Nai Nai said. "Bring someone home. It was his final wish." As New Year's loomed, Dai Ying finally hired Cheng, trading money to put on this show of love.

Cheng led her forward and pushed the courtyard gates open.

Across the entrance courtyard, near the open door of the living room, Nai Nai sat in a rocking chair. She looked like a fragile paper sculpture. Her skin was even more wrinkled than before, her hair white, no longer pepper grey like last year. The old woman tried to stand up, but her knees shook and she leaned back to steady herself.

Dai Ying ran to Nai Nai's side. "Be careful. Walk. Slowly." There was no trace of the firm-handed woman who had hit her with a feather duster for skipping classes or disobeying curfews, screaming that "hitting is caring, yelling is love." The beatings ruptured her skin, leaving scars that never healed completely.

Nai Nai's grip was light and shaky as they made their way toward the living room table.

"So you've finally found a boyfriend."

"I told you I would." Dai Ying gestured Cheng to come over. "This is Zheng Cheng. We were classmates. He runs an IT company for his family business."

"Lovely name. Gāo fù shuài." 高富帅 – tall, rich and handsome – three of the most valuable qualities for men, at least according to popular culture and Nai Nai.

"My father named me Cheng because he wanted me to be honest. Sincere." Somehow, he always knew the right words to say, the correct way to behave.

Dai Ying guided Nai Nai to her seat. "You should've eaten first instead of waiting for us." The old woman hadn't been well enough to cook in years. Tonight's dinner was prepared by a neighbouring auntie who did Nai Nai's housework.

"Wait. First, bring some food to your Baba. I set up a shrine in his old bedroom."

Dai Ying picked up chopsticks, laying fish and vegetables on top of rice, making the bowl so full that food threatened to fall off. Nai Nai should have told her about the shrine sooner; the old woman rarely shared anything with her and never even spoke more than a few words about Baba's passing. If she had known about the shrine's existence, she would have brought Baba a bouquet of lilies. She never got a chance to say goodbye to him, and there wasn't even a grave she could visit.

"Wipe your tears. You're not a child anymore. Bring Cheng with you and introduce him."

"But . . ." Wasn't it enough that she'd already bought Cheng home to meet Nai Nai? If Baba's spirit lingered near the shrine, he would see through their act. It was harder to lie to the dead than to the living.

"You still haven't paid your respects, so long after his death. Go. Now."

"Yes, let's go see your father. I want to meet him." Cheng gripped Dai Ying's shoulder and steered her toward the staircase.

Who did he think he was, pushing her around? But she didn't fling his hand off her shoulder, only squeezed her fist into a ball and kept walking. Nai Nai was still watching them, as if scrutinizing their bond, trying to judge whether Cheng would make a fine grandson-in-law.

Baba's shrine stood where his bookshelf used to be. There was no sign of his books in the room, collections and anthologies by the Misty Poets who grew up during the Cultural Revolution, a Lost Generation disillusioned by violence and social unrest. Hopefully, Nai Nai had only moved them elsewhere, not thrown them out like Dai Ying's old toys. If only she could sift through the books on his shelves. Read the pages of his poetry. Dig through the rubble and the cracks of the earth that had swallowed him.

On top of the shrine, a black-and-white portrait showed Baba in his forties, the frame surrounded by wilting chrysanthemums and white funeral candles. He scowled, his shoulders slouched forward, his hands stuffed awkwardly into his pockets. When had he last smiled?

Beside her, Cheng didn't even bother to glance at Baba's photo. He peered into a hallway mirror, smoothing out wrinkles on his shirt sleeves and straightening his tie.

"You should have gone to the bathroom instead of coming with me."

"And let Nai Nai get upset? I'm only doing my job."

"The perfect grandson-in-law."

He ran his fingers through his gelled hair, untangling knots. "No offence, but I'm only here because I need a holiday away from home. Plenty of girls would do anything to be my girlfriend."

"I wanted to come by myself."

"You should be more grateful for my help. No wonder you're single. No wonder you need to rent a boyfriend."

"Leave me alone," she snapped. "Go stand in the farthest corner."

She stood alone in front of Baba's shrine. As she leaned toward Baba's photo again, her head spun. The ground seemed to shake under her feet. Walls leaned forward as if about to crumble. Baba was gone, taken by the fault lines of the earth.

He had never talked back to Nai Nai, never mind lied like Dai Ying did now. He had never raised a hand against Dai Ying, never forced her to go against her will. If only he would chide her for being an immature disobedient daughter, yell at her for lying even after he had passed away. Anything would be better than the silence.

She laid the bowl of food in front of his photo. "Happy New Year, Baba."

Dai Ying poked at her rice with chopsticks as Nai Nai reached for more fish. It was still fully intact with its head and tail and bones, soaked in soy sauce, covered with red peppers and ginger slices, topped with finely chopped onions. The spicy aroma made her mouth water, but the fish head – with its bulging, unblinking eyes – made her throat tighten up.

Nai Nai placed a big chunk of fish into Dai Ying's bowl. "Eat."

"I'm not hungry."

"Don't be so picky. When I was your age, we were going through the Great Famine. Everything rationed. Only an egg on birthdays.

Eat fish, and you'll have a bountiful year." She picked up another piece and gave it to Cheng.

He devoured it immediately, then gave Nai Nai a piece of fish. "You eat too. Take care of your health." He selected two gigantic chunks for Dai Ying. "Nai Nai is right, don't be a picky eater. You've barely had any food."

She poked at the mountain of fish in her bowl. It was only her first night home, and they were already pairing up against her. Cheng might be skilled at playing his part, but she couldn't forget his words. *No wonder you need to rent a boyfriend.* Of course, he didn't understand – he wasn't the one who was being called a Leftover Woman and dragged to marriage markets.

She dumped all her fish into Cheng's bowl. "You eat it, since you like it so much."

"Don't be so rude," Nai Nai said. "Be gentler. Your future in-laws will be disgusted."

"I really don't want any. You eat."

Nai Nai gave more pieces of fish to Cheng. He wolfed them down.

Cheng raised his teacup in place of rice wine. He wished Nai Nai happiness as immense as the Eastern Sea. He wished her a life as long as the age of the Southern Mountain. The wishes were the same sweet greetings children always muttered to relatives, making adults grin and receiving thick red packets of money as rewards. Dai Ying scoured her brain for grander sayings, but couldn't remember any, and repeated the same lines half-heartedly.

Nai Nai returned the toast, wishing Cheng career success and Dai Ying marriage. Nai Nai never asked about her job. It didn't matter to Nai Nai that Dai Ying had gone to Shanghai as a migrant worker right after high school graduation; without the money, connections or the permanent residency status of the native Shanghainese, she had found a store clerk job and worked her way to a shift supervisor, planting roots for herself in the metropolis.

"Cheng, you're so xiào shùn. Dai Ying ought to learn from you."

Xiào shùn, 孝顺, filial piety, the chief of virtues, mandated that she paid visits to Baba's shrine, gave Nai Nai justifications for beating her and led her to rent a boyfriend. "I brought him home. Followed your wishes. Doesn't that count for something?"

"Cheng, you must thank your parents for letting you come visit us for New Year's."

His hands tensed around his chopsticks. He poked at three pieces of fish twice before picking up all the chunks simultaneously, then leaned forward to offer them to Nai Nai.

"I should meet your parents," Nai Nai said. "We must all have dinner together."

It was Cheng's turn to face Nai Nai's demands. "We totally should," Dai Ying said, grinning and elbowing Cheng. "His parents are looking forward to meeting you too."

His chopsticks slipped apart and the pieces of fish tumbled onto the cracked floor. "They're really busy." He reached for three more chunks of fish. "Eat, Nai Nai. Eat."

On New Year's Day, after Dai Ying and Cheng wished Nai Nai a Happy Year of the Ox, they all visited Baba's shrine again.

Dai Ying turned to Nai Nai. "I want to ask . . . what happened to his books?"

"They're too old and musty. I arranged for them to be boxed up."

Nai Nai was illiterate and didn't care much for the volumes, but they were Baba's most treasured possessions. Besides, Baba used to write her letters about once a month but never replied to her last one, where she complained about Nai Nai's increasing insistence that she get married. "Did they find any letters or notes from Baba in the end?"

"You should spend your time learning to cook better." The old woman reached for Cheng's arm, gripping it for balance. "Let me show you your father-in-law's books."

"You don't need to if it's too much trouble."

"It's important for you to be interested in scholarly pursuits."

Dai Ying had been the one who'd mentioned the books, but Nai Nai was turned away from her and grinning at Cheng. She praised him for his prestigious Beijing University degree, saying that he had a bright future ahead. Nai Nai led them both through a doorway near Baba's shrine, into a narrow attic filled with boxes.

Dai Ying opened up the boxes and dug through the piles. So many of his books, all musty, gathering dust and forgotten. She found a stack of his letters in an old box and could only read a few lines before she got teary-eyed. She put it aside and dug through the books until twenty minutes later, she found a battered anthology by Bei Dao. The father of Misty Poetry, known for his enigmatic work, his poems coded with unvoiced frustration and bitterness. Baba used to carry it everywhere, wrote notes in its margins and even scribbled half-composed poems in the endpapers. The cover was torn, the spine broken beyond repair. Pages fell out, covered with dirt, grime, ashes, stains that looked like blood.

She squeezed it tightly and took a deep breath. "It's his favourite book. He took it everywhere. Did they find this book among the rubble?"

"It's no use being sentimental," Nai Nai said. "It's not like the book can bring your Baba back. They should have spent more time digging for people rather than looking for this nonsense."

"You should've given it to me."

"If you like it, take it."

Dai Ying squeezed it again, feeling the rough fragile pages, the weight of holding on to words that had followed Baba until his final days. She guided Nai Nai downstairs to her rocking chair.

"Your Baba really wants you to find someone." Nai Nai swayed her chair back and forth, creaky and unsteady. "You two must get engaged. Dai Ying is already twenty-eight."

"*Only* twenty-eight." Her grandma was treating her like an ancient spinster again, a pearl yellowing with each passing moment. It wasn't enough that she had brought Cheng home, paid Baba respects and wished them a Happy New Year. She wanted to make Nai Nai grin and help Baba's spirit be at ease, but she couldn't utter a promise to marry lightly, especially with a fake boyfriend.

Cheng tugged his tie, playing with the tip until loose threads appeared. "We're not ready."

"Chairman Mao said that dating without intending to marry is fooling around."

"No, it's too soon," Dai Ying said.

Nai Nai slammed her fist down. "If you two are serious, then you should make a commitment!"

"Nai Nai, I need to talk to him. We're going for a walk." Dai Ying glanced down at Baba's book and reached for Cheng's hand, pulling him toward the exit of the courtyard.

Dai Ying led Cheng down an alley, clutching Bei Dao's poetry anthology. She couldn't stand Nai Nai's demands anymore. Even Cheng, a popular gāo fù shuài and a boyfriend-for-hire, was saying no to Nai Nai's request for their engagement. If only Baba were still alive; compared to the old woman, he would surely never be so demanding, no matter how much he wished her to find a boyfriend and settle down.

As she walked, she flipped through the pages of Bei Dao's book gingerly, one at a time, reading the poems until she found a loose piece of folded paper. It was thin and tattered, with worn edges. Baba's slant and curvy handwriting covered the page, smeared and fading. Her name was at the top.

Dear Dai Ying,

You asked in your latest letter what I really think about Nai Nai wanting you to get married. You mention your anger at her calling you a Leftover Woman. I'm sorry for the late reply. I have tried to write to you, but there's something I need to tell you that I'm not sure how to say. I don't even know if I'll send this letter.

I still remember how much you cried when your mama and I divorced. You were only thirteen then, when she left to remarry up north and I came to teach in Beichuan. But we didn't marry out of love, like your Nai Nai has led you to believe. She arranged my union with your mama, and the whole thing fell apart because we didn't want to be together. Forgive me.

Love and marriage are important things that you must carefully decide, for your own sake, not for mine or Nai Nai's. I trust you to make your own decisions.

Baba

Dai Ying grasped the paper tightly. It was comforting to see his familiar handwriting, but another part of her wanted to rip the letter into shreds. Why hadn't he told her the truth sooner, instead of going along with Nai Nai? After his divorce with Mama, he would always sigh in front of Dai Ying and rant about how much he missed Mama's cooking. He was too xiào shùn, living so long with someone he didn't like, and letting Nai Nai place the same pressure to marry on her, his own daughter. Nai Nai was worse. It's his final wish for you to get married, she said, all to manipulate her into dating.

Cheng peeked over her shoulder. "It's a letter, isn't it? From your Baba?"

She glared at him. He reached and snatched the letter from her hands, running off. She sprinted after him and yanked it hard from his hand. He pulled the letter toward him, trying to read it. The letter ripped, nearly tearing in half.

"Can't you just leave me alone? Look at what you've done!"

"Sorry." Cheng let go and stared down at the dirty cobblestones beneath him. "I was just curious."

She tried to piece the two parts of the letter back together, folded it gently and placed it back into the book. "Our act is over."

"But it's only New Year's Day. You agreed to hire me for the whole winter holidays."

She glared at him and at the battered anthology in her hands. The letter that was half-ripped, disintegrating. After reading Baba's letter, she couldn't continue the act the way he had.

"Nai Nai will just push you harder," he said. "Set up more blind dates."

"Probably."

"I'm sorry about the letter. Let me make it up to you. Let me talk some sense into Nai Nai."

"No, we're finished. I'll send your luggage back to you later."

"She'll get mad. She'll yell. Maybe beat you. I know, because my parents are like that too."

"Maybe you should go home and speak with your own parents, instead of avoiding it."

Pulling out her wallet, she took out payment for Cheng's work and flung the bills at him. Then she extended her hand and held it until he crushed it with a firm shake. He turned and walked away without looking back.

Dai Ying strolled down the narrow alley, walking one block to the riverside where the Yangtze flowed and intersected with two other rivers. Finally, she understood why Baba had gone away after his divorce; he must have gone to Beichuan to live near the fringe, to escape from Nai Nai and maybe even get away from Dai Ying, a child from an arranged marriage who reminded him of forced vows. And when he was teaching in Beichuan, a town in Wenchuan County, an earthquake struck. Cracks and gaps criss-crossed the fault lines, tearing the ground apart. The Beichuan Secondary School, where Baba was teaching, collapsed, burying a thousand students and teachers under concrete. Ashes scattered from the sky, burned eyes and mouths and ears, turned the town into a cemetery for the half-dead and the ghostlike living. The ground shook again, causing a landslide, tumbling rubble and remains into the roaring waters of the Yangtze River.

Where was Baba's body now? He could be floating nearby in the river, caught by the tide or lying in the depths. If she screamed his name, would he hear her voice calling him? He had brought her to this riverbank once, to fly a kite they had made together. Kites are harbingers of messages, he said, to express love vows, to make prayers, to murmur to the dead. She could make a kite and fly it for him, but what would she say? Should she tell him that she had received his message, scream at him for hiding the truth for so long or ask for the strength to speak with Nai Nai? There were no words to express her thoughts, no kite that she could fly.

Grasping Baba's book, Dai Ying stepped into the courtyard, longing to rip down all the crimson lanterns and banners. Maybe she could tell Nai Nai that Cheng had left because he was upset by Nai Nai's talks about the engagement. But Nai Nai would only snap at her for failing to keep a gāo fù shuài and losing out at the last minute. Then the old woman would visit the marriage markets and matchmakers again, searching for a boyfriend, as if shopping for a jacket for her to try on. And even if she were to find a real boyfriend, the questions "When are you getting married?" and "When are you going to have children?" would inevitably follow, as if she were a birth machine with the sole purpose of continuing the family bloodline.

Nai Nai waited for her in the living room, sitting in her rocking chair. She rose, knees shaking, and sank down, panting. "Why didn't Cheng come back with you?"

"He . . . went home."

"Did you upset him? What have you done this time?"

The lines that Dai Ying had rehearsed vanished. Nai Nai was frailer now, but could still hit her. A feather duster, the same one that the old woman had beaten her with when she was a child, hung across the room outside a cupboard, taunting the jagged scars on her back. The scars were faint now, barely visible, but still ached sometimes at night with unhealed pain, deeper than the cracks that remained long after an earthquake.

Dai Ying took a deep breath and whispered. "I hired Cheng. Paid him to be my boyfriend."

"What? Hired him?" Nai Nai swayed her rocking chair, banging wood against the floor. Firecrackers exploded in the courtyard outside. Cheerful folk songs blasted from the neighbours' TVs and radios, singing of grown-up children returning home and families reuniting around dinner tables. Nai Nai slammed her fist on the chair's wooden arms. "You lied to me." Her nails dug into the already torn surface, dragging uneven lines until the wood cracked and a sliver popped up, protruding sharply. "Leftover. Woman."

"What about all your lies about Baba?"

Dai Ying traced the torn cover of his book, gently thumbed through the volume page by page. Her hands found the letter, smoothed it out and clutched it tight, letting its edges dig into the lines of her palm. She read, mumbling and gradually raising her voice, vibrating the words off her tongue, as if solemnly reciting a will.

Nai Nai trembled, lips pursed together. "You're still young. You know nothing."

The old woman rose and headed for the stairs. Dai Ying offered her arm, but Nai Nai pushed it aside and fumbled up the uneven steps, one at a time, until finally reaching the top floor and walking over to Baba's shrine. From a jacket pocket, Nai Nai pulled out a photo of Ye Ye, dressed in an army uniform, and laid it beside the larger unsmiling image of Baba. Dai Ying had asked about her grandpa many times, but always got yelled at and sent to do housework.

"I only wanted your Baba to marry well. Want you to marry well. I was a foolish girl like you, long ago. Your Ye Ye and I used to be childhood friends who grew up together."

Nai Nai rambled on, explaining that she and Ye Ye had played with carved bamboo horses among lush plum trees. Her parents dismissed his request to court her because of his poor upbringing, but she had stupidly insisted on being with him. Then he went to fight in WWII, to win medals and prove himself worthy of her hand, and got himself killed. Her parents found her pregnant and cast her out as a shameful, ruined daughter. Neighbours slammed their doors against her. She had to pay for her stupidity, giving birth to Baba alone, without Ye Ye, her family or a midwife, aided only by a woman who helped her for her money.

"I don't want you to make the same mistake as me."

Dai Ying stared at Nai Nai. No wonder Nai Nai would orchestrate Baba's marriage and try to manipulate Dai Ying's own. But now, after knowing Baba's fate, Dai Ying could never go along with it.

"I'll leave Ye Ye's photo with Baba's. Maybe they could keep each other company."

Dai Ying nodded. Ye Ye, who was denied marriage with the one he loved, and Baba, so lonely and distant after a loveless union, never met in real life. Baba might rest easier with his father at his side, knowing that the old man too had died alone, far from home, lost among chaos and senseless violence.

Nai Nai tugged at Dai Ying's sleeves, and leaned on Dai Ying while they headed back downstairs. "You have to find someone, or you'll be frowned upon, laughed at, spat on."

"They shouldn't have mistreated you. It wasn't your fault."

After Nai Nai sat down, Dai Ying walked over to the stove and boiled water. She had barely eaten since yesterday and almost never cooked, but now she was famished, reaching for a pack of frozen tāng yuán, another dish that her family always ate for New Year's. These glutinous rice balls were oblong, unlike the perfect spheres Nai Nai used to make by hand, made round to resemble the circular unity of a family gathered together. Dai Ying dropped the frozen rice balls into the water, letting them sink and rise up, aimless balloons circling the pot.

"You're going to be alone," Nai Nai said. "There will be no one to take care of you."

Dai Ying stirred the pot with a spoon, poking the tāng yuán until one of them drifted toward the edge. A crack appeared on the rice ball, and sesame paste spilled out, turning the whole pot black. She filled two bowls and handed one to her grandma. Nai Nai took the bowl and slammed it on the table without eating. Dai Ying spooned up the rice ball that had split open. Sesame oozed out, steaming hot, burning her tongue, sinfully sweet. She swallowed it whole.

The Best Ham and Egg Sandwich on the Island

Sam Cheuk

LEGEND HAS IT THAT MR. LIU USED EGGS SHIPPED FROM Hokkaido, or that he waited for the Life Bread commercial bakery halfway across the city to open at five each morning to get the freshest batch. Others think he may have tossed some of the egg white away in a single motion between the egg's cracking and sizzling on the pan. To enrich the yolky aroma they say, though there's no verified eyewitness account of him doing so. The children loved him, as I did when I was a child, as with my older cousins, younger cousins and my cousins' kids. I don't remember his face at all, but I remember liking the sandwich.

No one would know the eatery was there if you're not from Pok Fu Lam, tucked away beside the village social club, with a barely legible sign. Until a foodie magazine published an article by another Gen-1.5er from my very own shantytown about the nostalgia for the simple sandwich, which was picked up by *Open Rice*, which led to a foodie Easter egg hunt – for naught, as it had by then moved to a shopping arcade uphill, and none appeared to have bothered to ask the village locals about where.

Around the bend before the sandwich place was the old man who owned the bigger of the two general stores in the village, always with a wall-mounted fan on him all four seasons, a white tank top tucked into cheap dress pants, usually with a belt, like every man over sixty used to do – with the exception of labourers, who'd roll the top above their potbelly during summertime. He was always chewing on a string of dried squid. "You want some?" he'd ask, whenever my cousins and I chased one another in some sort of game. "Now get outta here!" after we took a few strands out of his bag. In those days I would go there too to buy beer and cigarettes for the uncles (with the change left over I would buy a Schweppes cream soda and whatever candy caught my eye, and whichever uncle I was closest to post-delivery would smack me on the top of my head and joke, "You don't steal from a loan shark, you idiot!") who came over for card games and shot the shit, back in the village they grew up in, before they moved to the residential high-rises built above the shopping arcade uphill, or to another district on the island, or across the strait altogether.

Leon Lai used to follow one of the uncles as a triad initiate in the same village, before he somehow turned into a big name Cantopop star, my dad would tell me every time he saw his face on TV with fans yelling, "LEON, LEON, I LOVE YOU." I wondered then if Leon grew up there as well, had the same sandwich.

Seemed like back then I was always living in another era, or an era that was someone else's, or multiple eras happening simultaneously. Until I heard some students escaping into my village after a protest at a university nearby – they don't belong there. I wonder if they were chased out by the villagers, or welcomed into hiding. No one aside the locals knew how to get around the place; nothing is ever mapped out there except by rote. The cops probably wouldn't have entered anyway, can't exactly corner anyone in alleyways one adult body–width thick. Not even rival triads another generation back dared to enter our meek little village, with a single central entrance lined with fruit stalls. Not to say I am against the protests, but the students shouldn't have gone in there; not the attention the village needed. One of the last few villages left on the island that resisted developers' multiple attempts to buy out the whole hamlet – don't need to give the government any incentive to look into the matter. The house my grandpa built with his own hands is still there, for chrissake – it's history.

Ohh right, the sandwich. The secret behind the magic? It turns out to be butter. Mr. Liu buttered both sides of bread slices, fried the egg and ham in it. That's it. The butter sat in the butter tray, behind the sauté pan, open for all to see all those years. Some things just can't be seen 'til you remember to look for it. He made it that way because his wife used to take one to work each day, before her teeth fell out, but still savoured then that little bit of toasted crunch before incising her gum into bread. She never even cared for the ham, or so the story was told by the men who played mahjong in front of the social club no more. They weren't there the last time I visited anyway, I didn't recognize anyone and vice versa, should've gone uphill if it wasn't so late, it's not like it'd be slippery, it doesn't snow back home.

Red Egg and Ginger
Anna Ling Kaye

MEI ANSWERS THE PHONE CALL, THOUGH SHE KNOWS it will make things worse. "Baby's Full-Month Party," Mother says. "This weekend. Remember?"

Yes. Worse. Mei scrunches up to the wall next to her bed, her mobile phone threatening to slip from between her ear and shoulder. After the silence has gone on too long, Mei has to fill it with something. "What's the baby's name in the meantime?"

"Little Stinker."

"That's what you called me."

"And the hungry ghosts never came for you, right?"

Maybe not, but Mei remembers being confused as a child about why Mother thought she smelled so bad, no matter how well she washed.

Cousin gets on the line. Every sentence is an exclamation. "The banquet your mother's preparing, Mei! She's candying the ginger herself, dyeing the eggs! I'm so lucky she's here."

Mei imagines Mother sitting next to Cousin on Big Aunt's lacy couch, shaking her head to deny the compliments. If Mei wasn't so fond of Cousin, she would be jealous of all the attention she is getting. Mother's even moved in to Big Aunt's for the baby's first month, the better to help Cousin with her healing regimen. Papaya soup, wood ear tea, fish maw with black bean sauce. Mei taps a cigarette out of the box. She mouths the word "cousin" to S., who is lying across the bed from her. His combat boots and socks are neatly arranged on the floor. Looking at his bare feet, Mei realizes that even after all these months she can be caught off-guard by the near translucence of his white skin. The first time she'd seen those feet, she had traced the raised blue veins on them, marvelling at the tributaries. Blood tangible where hers is not. Now Mei busies her fingers with the cigarettes, the phone.

S. raises himself on an elbow. He points at Mei's stomach, and points at the phone. Mei shakes her head. She tries to focus on Cousin's happy chatter until Baby cries and Cousin needs to hang up.

S. doesn't understand Cantonese, but he can tell Mei didn't share her news with Cousin.

He asks why, forehead wrinkled, pupils widened into marbles of sea-glass green. When Mei asks for a light, he takes the cigarette out of her mouth and throws it out her window. They watch the white paper disappear down the shaft of grimy wall between Mei's building and the office tower ten feet away. Downstairs, the tram to Sheung Wan clatters by, bells warning jaywalkers out of the way.

"I'm sorry," he says. He drags a hand through his hair. Mei watches the brown curls spring back into coils. She used to love when that happened. But today, the hand, the hair, she wants to smack them. "I just want you to have support," S. says. "This is a big decision."

"She just had a baby," Mei says. "I'm a big girl. I can handle this."

* * *

The truth is, Mei can't afford to lose any more face to Cousin. "Your English is so good," Mother once said, soon after Mei graduated from university. "Why don't you work in private banking?" The next year, Cousin had done just that, graduating in accounting and landing a steady position at HSBC Finance.

Meanwhile, Mei had spent a few years trying to make it in performance art. Her grandest project was a piece for the anniversary of the 1997 Handover. This involved painting her practically naked body China-red with yellow stars and lying in front of the British Consulate with other fellow artists. It had been a costly statement: the press response was underwhelming, and soon after Father cut off Mei's monthly stipend.

"Get a nice job," Mother had said. "Get settled." By then, Cousin had just married a nice Cantonese bank manager.

"No one changes the world by managing money," Mei had shouted. She had moved out in protest. Soon, tired of the sleeping bags and mildewed towels of her equally destitute friends, Mei took a training position at Hype. She could approach hair as living sculpture, she decided. She would style hair to fund art, use art to fuel change. She always thought she would move to Italy by the time she was twenty-six, study mask-making and shape-shifting from the last inheritors of commedia dell'arte. Instead, Mei moved into the staff dormitory above Hype, a room shared with three other trainees. Her bed is an upper bunk with a curtain drawn across it for privacy.

Now, a year later, Cousin has delivered every Chinese grandparent's fondest hope: a healthy boy. Meanwhile, the only global impact Mei's achieved has been seducing Hype's star stylist from Montreal. Mei only ever addresses him by his nickname, "S." It was a tease to catch his attention at first, "s" for "syrup," as in maple, because that was all she knew about Canada. But now it marks him, sweet and stuck to her, available to no other. This makes the other salon girls cry into their pillows with envy. As for the latest news, only S. and Mei know.

S. gives Mei a brief, brave smile. His hand moves over the rubble of sheets, hesitating in the air between them. Then he rests it on her stomach, gently. The soft pat recalls Mother's hands soothing tummy aches. As a child, Mei used to close her eyes and pretend to still feel bad long after Mother's hands had accomplished their work.

"You're a bit happy, right?" S. asks. "Excited?"

"You're insane."

Still, Mei lets S. pull her close. She folds into the comforting warmth of her usual position in his arms – their first real touch since finding out.

The next day, on the subway train to Family Planning, Mei thinks about the quaintness of Full-Month parties. Back in the farming days, she could understand why waiting a month to name a child made sense. A baby surviving sickness and death that first crucial month would have been a good reason for all the ritual and celebration. But in modern Hong Kong, only unborn babies really need to be nameless. The shock of this thought thumps in Mei's chest. She turns to S., who is leaning against the glass doors of the train. His jacket is camouflage green, which just makes him more obvious against all the chrome and glass.

"I didn't like the way you threw my cigarette out yesterday," Mei says. "Those cost money, you know?"

Mei watches the apology surface in his clear eyes. It was this contradiction between his sensitivity and guerrilla gear that had first gotten her curious about him. She had wanted to know what made him laugh, what made him cry. Even now, riding the train to Family Planning together, she is fascinated by what she is learning about him every day. Charmed, even.

"Sorry," S. says. "I was stressed out. You know what they say about smoking and babies."

This is not what Mei wants to hear. "You think I'm not stressed out? That's why I needed a cigarette, right?"

He shrugs.

"If you can't deal with this, you don't have to come." Mei wishes her voice didn't sound so harsh, but she needs to be clear. "This isn't just a checkup, you know."

"Why isn't it?"

Mei sets her jaw and looks out the train window. What she'd love right now is that cigarette. And an egg tart, flaky with a sun of gold in the middle.

The counsellor's office is dark and smells like bleach. The narrow-faced woman behind the desk looks too much like Mei's mother: a tight perm crowding her face, her body rigid with efficiency. When the counsellor sees S.'s white skin, her eyes flicker into momentary confusion. She speaks to Mei in Cantonese. "Is this the father?"

"No," Mei says. "Moral support." In desperation, she adds, "He's gay." Mei's face warms.

The counsellor's mouth makes a tight line as she reads Mei's file. Mei almost expects the counsellor to say something like "your clothes are too tight." Instead, the counsellor asks how she can help. Mei asks, and the counsellor tells her the fetus has to be at least seven to nine weeks before there can be a procedure. The counsellor calls it a "termination." They will put a tube into Mei and suck the egg off her uterus's wall. It will hurt.

The worst part of the visit is the grainy ultrasound, where the counsellor locates a pulsating pimple in the green shadows that apparently represent Mei's womb. "Baby's heartbeat," says the counsellor, switching to English.

S.'s face blooms into a startled smile. "Wow."

Mei is surprised to see the counsellor smiling back at him.

Mei, who has to crane her neck from a reclining position to see the image, has a hard time believing it represents what's going on inside her. It is so two-dimensional. Monochrome. She shakes her head at the counsellor's offer to make a printout for home, and is mortified when S. asks for one in English. Mei is quick to wipe the cold goop from her stomach. She feels safer with her shirt pulled down again. The counsellor sees them to the door, presses the printout into S.'s hand.

Back in the bustle of the street, Mei decides to be upbeat. "She said fifty percent of pregnancies don't make it past the first three months. Maybe we should buy a big bag of pot, smoke it out of me."

S. laughs. "Or you could drink four gallons of water, and it will swim out."

"I know. Let's have a really great party, with some good music, and it will just dance out."

S. takes her hand in his, kisses the top of her wrist. "Or we could wait nine months. It'll slip out on its own."

Mei pulls her hand back.

He pulls the sleeve of her jacket, playful. "Come on, Mei. Think about it. I can support us all."

"I have a job too, you know." She swats his arm away. "We're not even married."

He drops to one knee with his arms thrown open. "Marry me then, Mei."

"I can't marry you." The indignation in her voice stops both of them. They face each other in the middle of the sidewalk, a pedestrian cursing at the obstacle. *Damn white ghost.*

S.'s face is a mask of goodwill. "So, really, you want to be a good Chinese girl. That's okay." He forces a smile, forces himself up. "I knew that about you."

She tries to be cute, rubs a finger on his forehead. "Let's see, under all this white, maybe you're really a nice Cantonese boy?" But the joke is too weak to make either of them feel better.

On the day of Baby's Full-Month party, Mei wakes with a sore chest. She takes off her nightshirt in the bathroom and checks her profile in the mirror. It is amazing to think of herself as pregnant. There is nothing different about her soft skin, her smooth stomach. Except her breasts feel different. They are stiff and sensitive in the hand. Mei imagines them swelling with milk, like water balloons, nature's prank on unsuspecting mothers. Mei decides not to consult the literature from Family Planning hidden under her mattress. She walks into the living room to look for her cigarettes.

Her roommate, Ching, is sitting on the couch in a long T-shirt and eating a bowl of ramen noodles. She has the Styrofoam bowl balanced on her bare knees, lifting it occasionally for a slurp of soup. The smell of salty broth fills the tight space, making Mei's empty stomach turn.

"Afternoon, bed-head," Ching says. "No work today?"

"I couldn't open my eyes."

"Romeo called for you. You are so lucky. I need love." Ching flicks a lock of burgundy-dyed hair out of her soup and gives a dramatic sniff. "I'm going to be alone forever. Not like you and Prince Charming."

Mei chews the unlit cigarette in her mouth and notices she doesn't want to smoke. In fact, the thought of smoking right then makes her gag. "You think he's a prince?" she asks. She tries to sound bored, keep the hope out of her voice.

"Of course," Ching says. "He's cute, he's got a good job, he adores you. He's tall too. He's the pot of gold."

Mei puts the cold cigarette on the table and looks at Ching. "So your mom would let you marry a white ghost?"

Ching's scandalized laughter is all the answer Mei needs.

To reach Big Aunt's home, Mei descends into the tight air of the downtown subway station, rocking under the harbour with other commuters. She emerges out of the ground in Kowloon, joining the evening shoppers flooding Nathan Road. The crowd forces her steps smaller, belching her into a clothing store where everything is child-sized. She can't show up at Little Stinker's party empty-handed.

The store is full of families: mothers, fathers, daughters and sons stumbling through a mess of strollers and diaper bags. A woman passes Mei, a child strapped to her front like a koala bear on a tree. The child's eyes are shut, its head burrowed into her chest. There is a sour smell on them, like old saliva.

Mei feels lost among the aisles. She touches the displays of tiny shirts and miniature socks, trying to envision a half-Chinese child in one of the pink anoraks studded with imitation rhinestones. It's all so wrong, even getting proposed to in the street like that. Mei had always thought there would be more of a story, something she could share at dinner parties. A hot-air balloon. A hike to the top of The Peak, Hong Kong's lights below like scattered sparks. Something involving the *Mona Lisa*. A pair of girls giggle nearby, their laughter tinny and annoying. Mei wonders why the sound also fills her with longing.

Mei is most drawn to the baby shoes. Each one is smaller than a credit card and fits snugly in the palm of her hand. She chooses a tough-looking pair of black hiking boots for Little Stinker. The idea of boots for babies makes Mei smile. Does a baby hike alone? Does a baby carry a tiny backpack and compass too?

Mei's mobile phone begins buzzing in her jacket pocket. It's S.

"I didn't see you on the floor this morning," he says. "Are you okay?"

Mei imagines him at Hype, hand cupped over the floor phone for privacy. No one even guessing the tedious ache of their recent conversations. Why Mei can't move to Montreal. Why Mei can't have his child and stay in Hong Kong. Why Mei can't give up the child and stay with him. The thought of S. having to act carefree and witty with Hype's fashionable clientele gives Mei a twinge of guilt. When he asks to meet later, she agrees. It will still be nice to see him after the stress of an afternoon with family. It will be excellent. They arrange to meet at the intersection nearest Big Aunt's building.

As Mei messages him the address, she realizes Cousin might not like the boots as much as she does. Cousin is more practical than that. Mei picks out a red velour jacket with the word "BOSS" stitched across it in big gold lettering. A brand name for Cousin, and ironic humour for Mei. It will complement the boots perfectly. Mei pays for both. She and Little Stinker, the least they can do is look cool.

Big Aunt's door opens very quickly, catching Mei in the middle of fluffing out her hair. Mei's latest do is the faux-fro, a jaunty poof that is all the rage in town. S. says it looks good on her, but declines one for himself, no matter how local it would make him.

"You look beautiful as usual," Cousin says. Her playful hands tease out bigger tufts in Mei's hair. "I can't wait for you to see Baby again. He's started smiling! It's great fun."

"Good thing," Mei says, "or you'd have had to return him to the baby store. You kept the receipt, right?"

Cousin laughs and darts down the hallway, looking behind once to make sure Mei is following. Motherhood has given Cousin a sheen of health. If she is ever commissioned to make a portrait of Cousin, Mei thinks, she'd represent her as a red-bean bun – a happy pastry puff with a shiny buttered crust. Herself she'd sculpt as a durian: heavy, spiky, guarding its offensive hidden fruit.

The living room is full of family. Even with the relatives milling about, the cacophony of small talk, Mother spots Mei's entrance instantly. Her conversation with Small Aunt uninterrupted, Mother glances from the clock to Mei's eyes. *Late, late, always late.* Mother's message conveyed without a word exchanged.

A sudden feeling of exhaustion overcomes Mei, but as she looks about for somewhere quiet to sit she sees Small Uncle has come up next to her.

"Hello, Uncle," she says, because she has to.

"Hello, Mei," he says. "Still doing art?"

"I work in a salon now." Where, Mei thinks, we could help you with that remarkable comb-over.

"The beauty industry, excellent. Are you in management?"

"Just training."

"Getting married soon?"

"No."

There is a pause before Uncle gives a thoughtless "oh," and moves away. It is a relief when Cousin reappears with a dish of candied ginger. Famished, Mei crams a piece into her mouth.

Mother's candy is wonderfully soft, the sugar crystals big enough to give it some grit, but small enough to melt on the tongue. The candy sweetness gives way to the fiery root beneath, and Mei holds it in her mouth without chewing. Ginger children bouncing up and down on her tongue until she can't take it anymore and spits them into her palm.

Mother descends on the girls, a platter of red eggs in her hands. The eggs are fresh from the pot, red dye still glistening and steaming.

"Ginger means more children," she teases Cousin. "You need to make a girl next year, a loyal ox to accompany her brother rat!" She turns to Mei. "And you, Ah-Mei. Little Stinker needs cousins to play with." Mother's eyes focus on Mei. "Why are you wearing so much makeup?"

Mei's hands rise instinctively to cover her face. "I'm not," she says.

Cousin rushes in a comment to cover for Mei. "It must be from the rush of the journey."

Mother thrusts the platter into Mei's hands. "Everyone gets an egg," she instructs. As she walks away, the cousins' eyes meet in mutual relief.

"I don't think I'm ready to have another baby," Cousin says. She gives a short laugh. "The stitches haven't even healed yet."

Mei remembers the scar after Little Stinker's delivery, a small angry mouth stretched above the sallow skin of Cousin's pelvis. Cousin had said an operation was the best way to have the baby, allowing her to get back to the bank at a predictable date. But looking at Cousin's weak body helpless on the hospital bed, Mei couldn't help feeling an incredible violence had been inflicted upon her.

Aunts, uncles and younger cousins pass by, grabbing eggs and ginger from the girls' plates, each outstretched hand accompanied by a perfunctory greeting. "Congratulations!" "Where's that cute little baby?" "Getting married soon?"

The younger children beg for a touch of Mei's hair. "It's like cotton candy," the littlest one sighs.

The girls field the stream of relatives with practised grace, smiling and nodding and giving short answers with just the right amount of information: too much means tedious follow-up questions; too little means painful drawn-out inquiry.

"Eggs and ginger. What you two need to be doing is feeding each other," says Big Aunt. Mother's older sister, Big Aunt, is what Mother would look like if she was fatter and happier. Big Aunt takes a piece of ginger and forces it into her daughter's laughing mouth. "The hot ginger gives a weakened new mother energy," she tells Cousin. The jade-ringed hands take an egg from Mei's plate. Big Aunt's quick fingers shuck the vermilion shell, revealing a trembling white meat underneath, streaked red where the dye seeped through. "And for you, Mei, you need the lucky red eggs to make you happy and strong for the future."

As Mei accepts the bite of egg, she looks into Big Aunt's broad face. The wrinkles bunched around her eyes can only have been formed from an excess of smiling. Sometimes, when Mother is deep in a tirade, Mei tries to hear the words in Big Aunt's gentle, supportive style. It helps her resist the urge to argue back. The egg slides slick on her tongue, easing the emptiness she's been feeling all day.

"When you were babies, you were our family's new hope," Big Aunt says. "Now the next generation brings even more joy."

The food in Mei's mouth turns to mush.

Then Big Aunt pulls Mei closer to her, speaks in a whisper. "Mei, I heard there's a magician stylist at your salon, young, from Montreal. Do you think he can help a frizz-head like me?"

Mei catches herself beaming. To be able to think and talk about S. openly in this room. "We're good friends," she says. "Though you're hard to improve upon, Auntie."

"Flatterer. I heard he's booked months ahead. But *Hong Kong Business Magazine* wants me to do a photo shoot at the new store next week and I thought I'd better get a spruce-up –"

There is a wail from the back of the room, and they all look up, alarmed. Following Cousin's eyes, Mei sees Baby raised in the air above a cluster of fawning relatives. The child's mouth is a black hole of sound, his face purple like he is about to pass out from the effort of screaming. When Cousin rushes over to take the screeching baby in her arms, Mei finds herself following. The three barricade themselves in a quieter room.

Big Aunt has converted Cousin's old room into a nursery, and the familiar walls feel welcoming after the smother of the family room. There is a window that looks down on the main street, and Mei walks over to it, enjoying the sight of ant-sized people scurrying underneath. She can see the intersection where she will be reunited with S., and marks the spot on the glass with her finger.

Hopefully they can at least watch a movie or share a meal before resuming the tense conversations of what to do next; if this is their end or new beginning. Maybe even share some wine. Mei had turned S. around on wine when she pointed out that the French seem to be fine drinking through pregnancy. "Okay," he'd allowed. "In moderation, though, right?"

Mei turns to Cousin, who is sitting on a new couch. The upholstery is covered with cartoon cherubs. The cherubs are cheeky, peeking down at Cousin's breasts, one nipple clamped in the moist circle of Baby's mouth. Between the two of them, Mei had a more impressive bust; it is something they always joked about when they went swimming as teens. Now Cousin has ponderous globes that Baby is vigorously applying himself to. Cousin's breasts are surreal epitomes of fertility, like they're out of some Botticelli painting. Mei can't stop staring, her newly tender chest chafing under the T-shirt.

Cousin gives a shy smile. "I didn't think it was going to work, at first. But Baby knew what to do. He started nursing right away." Cousin's voice carries an awed reverence, like someone who has witnessed a miracle.

All this frightens Mei. Cousin's tone, the sight of her and Baby still fused together, and especially the word "nursing." Mei lowers herself onto the floor next to them, at eye level with the scrunched face of the baby. His mouth twitches rhythmically; his eyes wide open and fixated on the air near Cousin's heart.

"Well, now we know what breasts are really for," Mei says. The platter of eggs she brought in is on the coffee table. Mei picks up an egg, enjoying the fit of it in her palm. "I'm sorry my mom keeps calling him Stinker," she says. "It is so annoying." Mei raps the egg against the tabletop. Cracks fissure the red shell.

"She's just being protective," Cousin says.

"From made-up ghosts?"

"Maybe they're real to her."

The peeled egg releases from its shell, its oily smell beckoning. Mei has been hungry all day, but nothing seems satisfying except these bland eggs. She sinks her teeth into the soft white mound.

Cousin looks at Mei. "You know what she said to me the other day? She said she hoped I would make a better mother than she is. She said she hoped Baby and I would be good friends."

"What can you say to that?" Mei asks. She is unable to meet Cousin's eyes, staring instead at the bowed baby's head, which has finally slipped free from the breast. His eyelids have lowered into closed flaps, newborn dreams flipping behind them.

"I said every parent is destined for failure. I said I accepted the failure."

"Um." Mei points to Cousin's bare breast, still hanging out of her shirt. Cousin widens her eyes in horror. They laugh as she rearranges herself.

Asleep, Baby looks like a beleaguered old man who has fought to be here, cheek smeared against Cousin's chest. Mei closes her eyes too, and in the darkness of her head, she smells them. Cousin and Baby. It is a comfortable smell, of warm skin and baby powder and clean clothes.

For someone who has only ever succeeded, Mei thinks, Cousin seems pretty smart about failure.

Just before the naming ceremony, Mei needs to vomit. With an apologetic smile, she pushes her way through the river of relatives, stumbles into the bathroom.

Hacking coughs force clear bile out of Mei's mouth. Each wave sends her knees digging into the spotless marble of Big Aunt's floor. The family counsellor had spoken about light nausea, but this feels like Mei's guts are trying to jump out of her body. Ginger sandpapers her throat. Her family's joyful cries come muffled through the door.

After Mei flushes away the evidence she feels much better. The purging leaves her almost refreshed. She takes her time washing her hands. Watches the suds build into small mountains of lather. Rinses under scalding water. Her hands come out red and scrubbed. The decisions she made at Family Planning were easy, but now her body's changing.

Mei checks the mirror again. She pinches her cheeks to bring back the colour. She bites her lips. As Mei straightens her T-shirt she passes her hands over the stowaway in her stomach. It embodies all the stolen kisses she's shared with S. in Hype's cramped storeroom, pressed tight against each other to avoid knocking the silver-pink rows of shampoo bottles from their shelves. All the plans S. and she conjured in their night walks along the churning dark harbour – fantasies of exploring western China by rail, watching the northern lights dance in the Yukon. He could teach the baby things he's tried to educate Mei about: Frisbee, blue cheese, ice-skating. In Montreal, there are even some good art schools to look into.

A knock on the door. Mother's voice calls her name. "What are you doing in there? Hurry up. The ceremony's about to begin." The door jiggles, and then Mother is inside the bathroom.

Mei curses herself for forgetting to lock it.

"What's this smell? What's happened?" Mother's nose is wrinkled in judgment, her head tilted back to smell better.

Braced for the reprimand, Mei keeps her face turned to the mirror. "I'm sorry. It's nothing. Maybe food poisoning."

"Poisoning? Now?" Hastily, Mother rubs her hands together to warm them, closes her eyes to concentrate. She puts one palm on Mei's stomach, another supporting her back. Energy courses between the two palms, spreading warmth up and down Mei's body. In the mirror, Mei is surprised to find that over the years she has become the taller of the two, the burr of her hair almost a foot above Mother's sooty perm.

"It can't be food poisoning. Your stomach is warm." Mother's eyes search Mei's in the mirror. Silence hangs between them like a bridge, neither of them finding the words to cross it.

"Well, I feel better now," Mei says. "Thanks."

Mother pushes Mei out the door. "Hurry up, we'll miss the announcement of Stinker's name."

They stand next to each other at the back of the noisy, laughter-filled living room, shoulders almost touching. Cousin's banker husband holds Little Stinker, who stares unblinking at the fan of people around him. Radiant, Cousin stands behind her husband, arms around his waist. With a flash of scissors, Big Aunt lops off a lock of Baby's thick hair and holds it in the air like a winning raffle ticket. The relatives all cheer and clap.

"Long life!"

"Great happiness!"

When Little Stinker's true name is announced, Mei glances over at Mother, and catches the wide smile on her face. Mei has grown up trying to capture these unprotected smiles, nestling them in her memory before the animated joy dies out of Mother's eyes. She leans over to her mother.

"I have something to tell you," Mei says.

Mother turns and meets her eyes, still laughing and clapping.

It is just a moment, but their shared silence is all Mei needs to let in the possibilities. She could quit smoking. She could keep the baby boots. She could go downstairs in a minute and say, "Martin, would you like to come up and meet my family?"

July Has Nothing to Do with Gods

Sheung-King

L

I STOLE SOMETHING OF YOURS. THIS IS THE FIRST thing he hears when he sits down. Children squeal as they run through the floor fountain that separates L – this shabby British pub – and the Tung Chung MTR station. "I stole something of yours," she says. "I'm sorry, but I can't say I regret it." This humid Friday evening in Tung Chung doesn't care about her confession. Others on the patio continue to chat. A group of cabin attendants, bros with loose neckties and perfectly coiffed hair, order another round of beer. "It's like a worm appeared inside my heart," she continues. "It's diving deeper every second, trying to get to the lowest point. But it doesn't know that my heart has no bottom. Inside my bottomless heart is a worm that keeps sinking. I know the only way to get rid of this feeling is to confess to you that I stole something of yours."

She didn't pick up his calls for an entire month. She told him she spent June on her own. In the evenings, after work, she would lie on her couch, scrolling through footage of the fights that broke out between protestors and the police, of the thousands of people, umbrellas in hand, marching through the streets of Hong Kong Island. Students in gas masks running away from tear gas.

"I understand if you're mad," she says. "So, I'll give you a deadline."

A deadline? The word "deadline" strikes him as odd. Why is this word allowed to combine time, space, life, action and urgency into one clear idea so naturally? The word almost doesn't make sense to him. He learned English as a second language; to study abroad he prepared for the IELTS exam by listening to hundreds of speeches by past American presidents. The IELTS test was expensive, so he studied hard, listened to the presidents' voices at night when he slept and, when he couldn't sleep, he played Obama's speeches in the background as he browsed through videos on Pornhub. Many times, he ejaculated to videos of strangers fucking to the deep yet soothing voice of the forty-fourth U.S. president. He passed the stupid test, which is designed not so much to teach people a new language but to make money; some marks were taken off, though, because he paused too much in the middle of his sentences.

"I'll be here next week," she continues. "You can tell me if you want to continue seeing each other then. And don't try to contact me in the meantime. I won't respond."

Cold silence fills the warm July air. He stares at the children, running around in the floor fountain. She was one of them once, an international-school student.

She places three one-hundred-dollar bills on the table and walks away.

Chinese public-school kids do not play in the fountain after school; they play the piano. He was a public-school kid, but he sucked at playing the piano. He could run, though. He represented his school in a number of competitions as a long-distance runner, even won some awards. Mindlessly racing forward was what he was good at, but his parents didn't care. Desperate for their son to be proficient in a European classical instrument so that they could look like competent parents to their friends, they had him learn the French horn, which required strong tongue movements but very little fingering.

UNIT 701

He sits on the toilet again – still, he cannot shit. This has never happened to him. He's twenty-six, always had healthy bowel movements. He hasn't worked in almost six months. In his free time, he exercises regularly and maintains a balanced diet.

Giving up, he starts going through the stuff in his bedroom: the stash of weed tucked under the mattress, the stack of cash in the mooncake box in his underwear drawer and the orange butt plug under his bed are all where they're supposed to be. He checks the login history on all his social media accounts – nothing unusual. Not that he has a high limit on that HSBC VISA card of his – he's unemployed, and she, though he doesn't know what her job is, lives in a penthouse. Nonetheless, he quickly goes through his credit card history anyway – no suspicious transactions either.

He sits back on the toilet.

"Constipation" sounds a little like "simulation," which reminds him of the word "assimilation," and the word "assimilation" makes him think about the sex he's been having with her for the past two months. She's always the one who initiates, who comes over to his place, knowing exactly what she wants. He enjoys how little control he has when she's on top, riding him, enjoying herself. "You're a good boy," she says, putting a blindfold on him and tying his arms to the bed. She often slaps him and even chokes him without warning. This lack of agency is the freedom he actively invites.

He's hard. Constipation, arousal, confusion and a vague sense of loss are all coming together naturally.

"便秘" (bin6 bei3) is "constipation"; "便" on its own, means "easy," "informal," "ordinary" and "comfort." "秘," on the other hand, means "secret." The words "便秘" describe this moment better than any English word he knows.

He stands up and ejaculates into some toilet paper.

WET MARKET

Despite being 便秘, he wakes up the next morning feeling extremely hungry and heads to the wet market downstairs for some steamed buns. It is early, not even 7:00 a.m., but standing in line are cabin attendants, waiting to get a decent breakfast before departing the city.

Not too long ago, he was one of them, a cabin crew member. Relatively tall and capable of speaking good English, he was hired by Cathay Pacific right after graduating from UBC with an economics degree. He flew back and forth between Hong Kong and Vancouver for two years before losing his job due to flights being cancelled during a recent pandemic.

"What do you like most about flying?" This is the first question she asked him when they met. "Your profile said you work for Cathay."

After filling his stomach with siu mai and barbecue pork buns, he decides that he needs some fruit to deal with his indigestion.

UNIT 701

Central, though only twenty-odd minutes away by MTR, feels distant through the screen. For cabin attendants, all images of the outside world during the twelve-hour flight exist only on small TV screens that play trashy Hollywood movies in front of passengers. The screen in front of his treadmill has the word "live" in the top right-hand corner. Protestors are occupying one of Central's main streets.

He looks outside. Tung Chung is perfectly quiet.

MTR

The MTR station downstairs is completely destroyed. Unable to shit, he goes for a late-night run, only to find police officers in all-black riot gear patrolling the scene. No protestors. The entrance gates are broken, glass is scattered all over the ground and the ticket machines are smashed to shambles. His stomach starts growling. The blood in his body turns cold. He starts walking away from the station, through the pedestrian tunnels and underground biking lanes, all the way to the riverside, where the Ngong Ping 360 gondola lifts that take tourists to the Tian Tan Buddha during the day hang above the river. Staring up at the lifts, he no longer feels like he's in Tung Chung, but inside a larger organism, that all the stillness that surrounds him is part of a system giving mobility to something larger. But what that thing is, he cannot tell.

"I stole something from you," she'd said.

When a person is born, the brain starts comprehending the world by telling itself stories. The adult brain will sometimes convert to religion because, to the brain, religion works the same as childhood memories do. Take Christianity. The opening book of the Bible, Genesis, tells a story that explains how the world came to be, using not logic but narratives derived from a number of religions in the same geographic area that perpetuate a set of ideologies. Since narratives in religious texts are stories used to promote a set of ideas, for those who were raised Christian, narratives in the Bible become a set of principles through which to interpret the world.

But the human brain is frail, and even for those who are not religious, sometimes in adulthood it becomes so tired that it wants to reboot, returning briefly to the point of its childhood memories, its basic principles. At these moments, religions (and sometimes cults) hack in.

Running will disrupt the workings of this larger thing.

He runs along the riverbank, passes by an Indian restaurant near the pier. His stomach is bloated. His back is sweaty. But breathing becomes easier as he runs. He runs around a large square surrounded by white, concrete, private apartment buildings with green window frames. In the centre of the empty square is an open area where children play during the day. Surrounding this play area are shops: a 7-Eleven, a small drugstore, a German restaurant, a supermarket, a Thai restaurant, a kindergarten and a hair salon. He runs around the circle, passing each shop four times, and decides to enter the park next to the Tung Chung Novotel, where pilots and cabin crews stay during their time in Hong Kong. He runs past a pagoda where the elderly practise Tai Chi in the morning. He doesn't stop. Lights in the buildings that surround him start to turn on. Thousands of eyes from the window might be watching him as he sprints through the park, but he doesn't care. So what? Let them watch. He starts racing toward the airport.

"It's as if a worm appeared in my heart," she'd said to him. What did she steal? Thinking about this makes everything around him become unfamiliar. He sees reality's interface flash across his eyes, quickly refreshing, contrasting into a set of fundamental principles, before expanding and re-becoming the reality he is familiar with.

He returns home and shits.

The next morning, he wakes up extremely hungry. He hears the beeping of Octopus cards on his way to the wet market. The

MTR station – destroyed the night before – is now in perfect condition. People with suitcases in hand and purses on their shoulders are leaving Tung Chung for Central to go to work. The ticket machines that were smashed to pieces just last night are now fully functional once again.

It's as if, last night, a moment that belonged to another time, had randomly inserted itself into his present.

DEADLINE

Next week at L, he asks her: If there were a machine that could simulate reality to a point where one could perceive and understand everything as reality itself, would she enter it? After a moment of silence, she tells him that yes, she would, but only if one thing about the world might be changed. What that one thing is, she does not tell.

"I'm tired," she says. "If you've decided to forgive me, we're going back to yours."

L

She has handcuffs with her this time. She takes out the orange butt plug he hides under his bed.

"How did you know that was there?"

She rubs lubricant on the butt plug and starts fingering his anus and in one swift movement, inserts the butt plug. He squeals. But despite his having felt a sudden shot of pleasure, his penis remains flaccid, which has never happened to him before.

"Are you okay?" she asks.

"I'm sorry," he says.

"Are you still thinking about what I stole?"

He doesn't answer. But the truth is that he doesn't care about what she stole. It's probably something that never belonged to him in the first place. All he can think about right now, lying face down on his pillow, with the butt plug still up his ass, is the Tung Chung MTR station that was completely destroyed, and the police in riot gear patrolling the scene. The same station was fully fixed and functional the morning after. He tries to stop thinking about the station, but Tian Tan Buddha sits above him, watching, in the mountains above Tung Chung, making sure that this, and not anything else, is all he can think about at this moment.

"Don't be sorry," she says. She pulls out the butt plug and tosses it aside. For a while, they lie there in silence.

"I want to live in a world that is completely secular," she says. "If that's not possible, I need to make sure that, at the very least, Christianity does not exist." She sighs. "I think raising your child religious is a form of child abuse. Why are we allowed to pressure an immature mind to live in line with a set of beliefs without consent?"

She opens the blinds next to the bed. In some of the apartments nearby, people are watching TV. Lights from their TV screens flicker.

"If I continue living in this world," she continues, "my existence will be completely reliant on me being in opposition to the things I hate. It's tiring."

They lie down. The MTR station downstairs with its red-and-white logo shines brightly through the window, into the bedroom and onto their faces.

"Let's not consider it a religion," he says.

"What do you mean?"

"I learned this recently. Genesis has nothing to do with God. It is just a description of a childhood memory, a detailed account of a mind trying to understand and comprehend components the world is made up of, things like light and darkness, sky and ground, the names of plants and animals and so on. It has nothing to do with the creation of the earth. It's a description of a learning curve, structures that a mind is inventing to make sense of how things in the world work."

He is right. Genesis has nothing to do with God. It is a description of a mind, telling itself a story, creating narrative structures – memories – to understand a world that is already there.

The orange butt plug sits next to the window. Lights from television screens of apartments nearby continue to shine through. A plane takes off.

Foggy Days, Foggy Ways

Lydia Kwa

VANESSA KNEW SHE WAS SUPPOSED TO LEAVE, BUT something was keeping her here. She gazed wistfully at the front windows of her family home. All the lights were out. Her parents and twin brothers would be sound asleep at this late hour. It was deserted on the street. She floated up the path dividing the front garden plots. The beds were barren except for a few cabbages and twigs scattered about to deter neighbourhood cats from peeing on the soil. She'd been the one who did that, before she got sick. She'll miss doing her share of gardening in the spring and summer. Vanessa slipped through the door and into the house, pausing just for a few moments in the living room to listen – she could hear her family breathing as they slept. Even the house breathed. One of the perks of being dead: she heard in ways she never could before.

She looked in on Sebastian and Mikey. On their separate beds, their legs were wrapped around bolsters – Sebastian's had a Doraemon cover; Mikey's was Pokémon. She went up to breathe lightly on each face. Sebastian smiled whereas his twin's nostrils flared.

She ventured into her parents' room. Her mom tossed restlessly and cried softly in her sleep while her dad snored, flat on his back. Vanessa couldn't tell if he was sad.

Next, she headed to her bedroom. Everything looked the same. Backpack on her chair. Desk tidy. Made sense, since it was only that morning when she'd died. Where was her school uniform, though? She vaguely recalled being rushed to the hospital the week before.

Vanessa looked fondly at the twelve plushies on the bed. She lay down on the bed and snuggled up to Moxie, the tiny turtle with the extended eyelashes. What were her parents going to do with her friends? Vanessa could tell that Moxie was a little sad too. They'd been together for the past six years, ever since she was three. She whispered to Moxie, "I don't want to lose you."

She got up from the bed and returned to the living room and hovered next to the IKEA floor lamp, the one that was all crinkly, off-white paper. Her parents bought it because it reminded them of paper lanterns they used to play with as kids growing up in Singapore. She'd gone to Singapore with them, just that one time before her twin brothers came along. That was where she found Moxie, in a store at Parkway Parade. Or rather – it was Moxie who'd called out to her.

Vanessa wished she could tell her mom a few things, but that was impossible now. She drifted into the kitchen and stared at the whiteboard on the side of the fridge. Her eyes narrowed as she studied the invoice from a funeral home. It had her name on it and stated the time of cremation, three days from now. She felt a bit woozy.

She rushed into the bathroom. Although it was totally dark in there, Vanessa could see herself in the mirror on the cabinet above the sink. She stared at the hole in her throat, a scar from the intubation at the hospital. What was going to happen when her body was cremated? Would she be released from this in-between state?

There were just no answers; but she suspected that she needed something, some gesture that would assuage her restlessness.

It was almost 5:00 a.m. when she left the house. Guess she needed to hang around in the home, see how everyone was. Maybe they didn't catch it from her, or if they did, they seem to have recovered. She sighed with a mix of sadness and relief.

She went to Gaston Park across the street and sat down on a bench. She felt lonely. Time lost its meaning without all the activities of being with her family and friends. She worried about the cremation. As the fog thickened around her, she was lost in her inner fog of confusing feelings and ruminations.

The light made a feeble attempt to pierce through at sunrise. There were faint traces of humans and dogs in the far corner of the park. She wasn't too worried about being spotted by the humans, but the animals might sense her presence. She would move away if the animals came any closer.

Vanessa turned in the direction of a luscious-sounding, operatic voice. The singer was walking toward the park, from half a block away, swinging her arms vigorously at her sides. The Malay song was familiar, a song about a white cockatoo on a windowsill watching an old woman with only two front teeth left. Vanessa smiled.

The voice drew closer, then passed by the bench where Vanessa sat. There were many Asians in the neighbourhood, but it was the first time she'd ever heard someone other than her mom sing "Burung Kakak Tua." What a badass delivery – this auntie didn't seem to mind that there were others around who could hear her.

The auntie strutted up and down the length of the park, her blue surgical mask like a flag waving at Vanessa from her wrist. She was definitely older than her parents. She started to do a kind of funky chicken dance while she sang. "Burung kakak tua, hinggap di jendela, nenek sudah tua, giginya tinggal dua."

Vanessa decided she would follow along. She was cautious at first, hummed very softly, then she got bolder and joined in, floating behind the auntie, swaying from side to side. She imagined that white cockatoo perched on the window watching the old woman in the room. She had always wondered what the relationship was like between the two, but the lyrics didn't really give much of a clue.

She loved the refrain, "Letrum, letrum, letrum, oo la la," though she had no idea what this meant. She always got this line wrong. Her mother stopped trying to correct her, and it became their inside joke. She sang her version, "De boom, de boom, de boom, tra la la."

The auntie came to a halt and turned around. "Who's following me?" She squinted into the fog.

Vanessa felt nervous and thrilled at the same time. So far, in the twenty-four hours since she'd left her physical body, no other human had noticed her. This auntie must be special. She drew closer and spoke in a timorous voice, "Auntie, can I ask you a favour? I need your help."

"You lost? Aren't you supposed to be in school? Why is your voice so soft?"

"School was where I got sick. It's why I'm not going back."

The woman frowned. "Your parents okay with that?"

That was impossible to answer.

"Eh, Auntie. I have something to tell you, but I don't know if it will spook you."

"Hey, you got same accent, like me!"

Vanessa brightened up. "Yes! My parents grew up in Singapore, but I was born here."

"Come a bit closer. I can't see you so clearly." The woman waved her hand at Vanessa and put her mask back on.

Vanessa floated closer until she was about two feet away.

"What's your name?"

"Vanessa," she answered. "And you, Auntie?"

"Call me Auntie Geok, can."

"Auntie Geok, nice to meet you. This song is one that my mom taught me."

The woman nodded approvingly. "You live in the neighbourhood, right?"

Vanessa nodded, feeling awkward again. She wasn't really living, but what could she say?

"Wah, you not wearing mask. I suppose it's okay, given we are outdoors. Don't know if fog make difference to virus transmission."

"Don't worry, Auntie. I can't infect you because I'm already, uh, gone."

"What do you mean, gone?"

There were really no words she could use, so she might as well show Auntie. Vanessa pointed to the hole in her throat. Maybe the fog had rendered it more difficult for Auntie Geok to notice it. Auntie Geok squinted hard at where Vanessa pointed. "Eh, what happened there?"

Maybe she had to give Auntie Geok a stronger hint. "Hospital. They put a tube in me to help me breathe. See, I still got the blue gown on."

Auntie Geok's eyes bulged as she covered her mouth with one hand as she took a sharp intake of breath and gasped. She straightened up and quickly pulled her right earlobe twice, backing away.

"Aiyah! You, you are not . . ."

"Please, Auntie. I need your help." Vanessa stayed rooted to the spot, lost in the fog as the woman walked briskly away.

The recess bell rang. Soon the preschoolers would stream into the park. Vanessa didn't want to take a chance someone else could see her, so she scooted off to the smaller park nearby. She looked at the row of trees up on the slope. She went to the one she liked best and rested against it, considering what to do next. She looked up at the bare branches. The buds were just beginning to show. Flowers would arrive once the weather warmed up. She moaned – things just weren't the same anymore. She thought about what had happened. Auntie Geok must have mistaken Vanessa for a pontianak. She felt anguished and lonely. Maybe the tree understood just how awful she felt. She cried tears that evaporated quickly into the fog.

From the stories her mom used to tell her, pontianak were female vampires who needed to feast on the freshly harvested entrails of male humans. Pontianak had been women and girls who had died violently as a result of being betrayed by the ones they loved. Vanessa pouted. No one had betrayed her. She wasn't keen on eating any entrails. Never liked them when she was alive, and her tastes hadn't changed.

She put that doubt to rest. Whatever she was called, she was in-between, restless and needing something, before she could be released from this current predicament.

Her recollection of the past week was hazy. Things had happened so quickly. She had felt feverish, quickly developed a sore throat. Last thing she remembered at school – her body collapsing, just as she got up from her desk. She couldn't breathe. The classmates cleared out of the room. Sounds of the ambulance siren. Hands that lifted her up on a stretcher.

When she regained consciousness, she was hooked up to machines. She had a tube in her throat. It hurt so much to breathe. Her throat felt as if stabbed by a hundred tiny knives. She lost track of time. She glimpsed the faces of her parents and twin brothers through a FaceTime call. She heard the word "COVID" pronounced to her family by the doctor in attendance, suited up like he was going to travel to some distant galaxy.

She worried that her family would get sick too. The fire that wracked her body seemed interminable, but it was later followed by a numbing coldness. Then a long beeping sound, and a flat, neon-green line on the machine. Hands on her, cold gel on her chest followed by several sharp electrical shocks. A rough, gurgling sound came out of her throat. She left her body, floated above, then passed through the windows.

So that was what dying felt like. She drifted aimlessly for quite a while before deciding she would go home.

Vanessa snapped out of her recollection and looked around her. A boy rode his bicycle on the path below. A woman was walking behind, keeping an eye on him. The boy went out of Vanessa's view but returned soon enough. He must have gone around the circular path. Seemed like such an ordinary thing to do, when you were a kid. Now, having crossed over, she definitely had no patience for going around and around, stuck in this transient state. This was not fun, nothing like riding a bike. She wanted to go wherever she was supposed to. She supposed this meant going eventually into the next reincarnation, from what her parents had told her.

An idea came to mind. That night, she went home again. She lay on her bed and told Moxie her plans. She was about to leave the house when she heard the sounds of whimpering coming from her parents' room. She was surprised to find her dad's face streaked with tears, as he whimpered. She had never seen him cry before. He must be sad that she was dead. It shook her up, reminded her that Dad loved her too.

The next morning, it was still foggy. Vanessa lost track of how many foggy days there had been. She waited at the same bench at Gaston Park. People and animals started showing up. She was nervous – what if Auntie Geok didn't come? Vanessa felt her throat tense up when she spied Auntie Geok's form through the fog.

"Is that you, little ghost?"

Vanessa floated up from the bench, slightly elated. "Yes, it's me, Auntie! You can still see me. I was hoping..."

"Yah but you a bit blur. Uh, I don't mean that other kind of blur, huh," the woman interrupted herself, sounding a bit embarrassed.

Vanessa laughed. "True, Auntie, I am a bit blur these days, ever since I died."

"Okay, sorry lah, I got scared of you and ran away yesterday. But today, I was hoping you'd come back and tell me what you need."

"You're kind, Auntie."

Auntie Geok gestured to Vanessa with a wave of her left hand. "Come, walk with me."

"Can I, uh, float near you?"

Auntie Geok nodded, her facial expression all serious.

After the walk, they returned to the bench. Vanessa told Auntie Geok about her parents and twin brothers. She said her parents were going to have her body cremated the day after, so could Auntie please pass a message to them today?

"This what they call time-sensitive." Auntie Geok's plucked eyebrows lifted, like cranes preparing for flight. "Can write on paper and put under the door? Because I don't want them to come kachau me afterward."

Vanessa nodded. A note, the old-fashioned way, sounded like a plan.

Auntie Geok rummaged in her jacket pockets and produced a small spiral-bound notebook and a ballpoint pen. "Okay, you say, and I write."

Vanessa composed the note, stating what she needed from her parents. "Oh, can you please add that I always used to sing 'de boom, de boom, de boom, tra la la' on the song 'Burung Kakak Tua'? Then my parents will know for sure this note comes from me."

Auntie Geok nodded approvingly. "Smart."

Vanessa led Auntie Geok to their house. There might be another half hour before everybody would head out. Auntie went up to the front door and slipped the note into the mail slot before running away.

Two days later, the fog lifted. The sunshine was glorious. Vanessa wanted to say goodbye to Auntie Geok. She went to Gaston Park for the last time and looked around. Where was she? Vanessa felt slightly panicked because she didn't have much time before she had to leave. Then she heard Auntie Geok's bold singing voice across the street. Vanessa sneaked up behind Auntie Geok and blew a soft current of air at her left ear. Auntie Geok shivered then turned slowly around.

"You! Still here?"

"I came to say goodbye," Vanessa said. "I can leave now because thanks to you, I got what I wanted. See?" Vanessa stretched out her arms, holding her companion out to show Auntie Geok.

"Ah," Auntie nodded, "so that's Moxie. Glad your parents respected your wish." Auntie Geok blew air kisses at Vanessa and Moxie. "Bye-bye, sweeties. Safe journey."

Editor's Note

Thanks to the contributors for their support. Their belief and commitment made this book possible. Connie Woo helped with the translation of "Lonely Face Club"; Annie Jin and Wan Liu clarified many points as well. Thanks to Ashley, Jen, Noelle and Paul.

Contributor Biographies

EDDY BOUDEL TAN writes stories that depict a world much like our own – the heroes are flawed, truth is distorted and there is as much hope as there is heartbreak. He's the author of two novels: *After Elias*, a finalist for the ReLit Awards and the Edmund White Award for Debut Fiction, and *The Rebellious Tide* (Dundurn Press). In 2021, he was named a Rising Star by Writers' Trust of Canada. His short stories can be found in *Joyland*, *Yolk*, *Gertrude Press* and *The G&LR*, as well as in *Queer Little Nightmares: An Anthology of Monstrous Fiction and Poetry* (Arsenal Pulp Press). He lives in Vancouver with his husband where he is currently writing his next novel while listening to the language of birds from his balcony.

Winner of the 2019 *Vallum* Poetry Award and the 2020 Power of the Poets Contest for their ekphrasis of Abbas Akhavan's *variations on a landscape*, ELLEN CHANG-RICHARDSON's multi-genre work has appeared in *Augur*, *Canthius*, *The Fiddlehead* and more. A settler of Taiwanese and Chinese Cambodian descent, Ellen currently lives/works on the traditional unceded territory of the Algonquin Anishinaabe (Ottawa, ON) where they co-curate Riverbed Reading Series and write collaboratively as part of the poetry collective VII. They are the author/co-author of six poetry chapbooks and an editor for *long con magazine* and *Room*. Their debut collection is forthcoming with Buckrider Books in Spring 2024.

SAM CHEUK is a Hong Kong–born Canadian author of *Love Figures*, *Deus et Machina* and *Postscripts from a City Burning*. He is currently working on *Marginalia*, which examines the function, execution and generative potential behind censorship.

ANNA LING KAYE is a writer and columnist. She has served as artistic editor at *PRISM international* and *Ricepaper* magazines, and guest editor at *The New Quarterly*. Kaye's fiction has been a finalist for the Journey Prize, CBC Short Story Prize and PEN Canada New Voices Award, and won the RBC Bronwen Wallace Award. A third-culture kid of mixed-heritage, Kaye is grateful to live in Vancouver on the traditional and unceded homelands of the Musqueam, Squamish and Tsleil-Waututh Nations.

LYDIA KWA has published two books of poetry and four novels. Her fourth novel, *Oracle Bone*, was published by Arsenal Pulp Press in 2017 as the first novel in the chuanqi 傳奇 duology. A new version of *The Walking Boy* was released in Spring 2019 (Arsenal Pulp Press). Her next novel, *A Dream Wants Waking*, will be published by Buckrider Books, an imprint of Wolsak & Wynn, in Fall 2023. She lives and works on the traditional and unceded territories of the Coast Salish peoples, known by its colonial name, Vancouver.

SHEUNG-KING (Aaron Tang)'s debut novel, *You Are Eating an Orange. You Are Naked* (Book*hug Press), was a finalist for the

2021 Governor General's Award, a finalist for the Amazon Canada First Novel Award, longlisted for CBC's Canada Reads 2021 and named one of the best book debuts of 2020 by the *Globe and Mail*. Born in Vancouver, Sheung-King grew up in Hong Kong. His work examines "the interior lives of the transnational Asian diaspora" (Thea Lim, *The Nation*). He taught creative writing at the University of Guelph. He now teaches at Avenues: The World School, Shenzhen. His next novel, *BATSHIT SEVEN*, will be published by Penguin Random House Canada in 2024. He holds an MFA in creative writing from the University of Guelph.

ISABELLA WANG is the author of the chapbook *On Forgetting a Language* (Baseline Press, 2019), and her full-length debut, *Pebble Swing* (Nightwood Editions, 2021), shortlisted for the Dorothy Livesay Poetry Prize. Among other recognitions, she has been shortlisted for *Arc*'s Poem of the Year contest, *The Malahat Review*'s Far Horizons Award and Long Poem Contest and was the youngest writer to be shortlisted twice for *The New Quarterly*'s Edna Staebler Essay Contest. Her poetry and prose have appeared in over thirty literary journals and three anthologies. An editor at *Room* magazine, she also works for *poetry in canada* and Massy Books, and directs her own non-profit mentorship and consulting business, 4827 Revise Revision St. (iBella Inc.).

YILIN WANG (she/they) is a writer, poet and Chinese-English translator who lives on the unceded lands of the Musqueam, Squamish and Tsleil-Waututh peoples (Vancouver, BC). Her writing and translations have appeared or are forthcoming in *Clarkesworld, Fantasy Magazine, POETRY, Guernica, Words Without Borders, The Malahat Review, Room, CV2* and elsewhere. She is the editor and translator of *The Lantern and the Night Moths*, forthcoming with Invisible Publishing, which features her translations of work by five modern and contemporary Chinese poets. Yilin has won the Foster Poetry Prize, received an ALTA Virtual Travel Fellowship and has been a two-time finalist for the Far Horizons Award for Short Fiction. She has an MFA in Creative Writing from UBC and is a graduate of the 2021 Clarion West Writers Workshop.

DAN K. WOO's family came to Canada in the 1970s. His grandfather was a fire captain and the first firefighter to die on duty in British Hong Kong, partly as a result of the British colonial system. In 2018, Woo won the Ken Klonsky Award for *Learning How to Love China* (Quattro Books). His writing has appeared in such publications as the *South China Morning Post*, *Quill & Quire*, *China Daily USA* and elsewhere. A Toronto native, he lives with his partner in the city and writes in his free time.

BINGJI YE came to Canada from Northern China. With majors in international business and economics, she graduated from Hebei University of Economics and Business and the University of Alberta. A poet, novelist and educator, Bingji wrote poems and stories for Chinese language media in Canada. Her first novel, *The Trap of Yves Saint Laurent Scent*, was published by one of China's biggest publishers in 2006. The novel is about romance, conspiracy and commercial war. She has lived in Edmonton, Regina, Ottawa and the Greater Toronto Area with her family.